WILD & CHANCE

THE PUPPY WAR

WILD & CHANCE
THE PUPPY WAR

BOOK 2

ALLEN ZADOFF

LITTLE, BROWN AND COMPANY
New York Boston

Little, Brown and Company
Hachette Book Group
1290 Avenue of the Americas, New York, NY 10104

Visit us at LBYR.com

Originally published in hardcover and ebook by Little, Brown and Company in May 2021
First Trade Paperback Edition: April 2022

Little, Brown and Company is a division of Hachette Book Group, Inc. The Little, Brown name and logo are trademarks of Hachette Book Group, Inc.

The publisher is not responsible for websites (or their content) that are not owned by the publisher.

The Library of Congress cataloged the hardcover edition as follows:
Names: Zadoff, Allen, author.
Title: The puppy war / by Allen Zadoff.
Description: First edition. | New York : Little, Brown and Company, 2021. | Series:
    Wild & Chance ; book 2 | Audience: Ages 8–12. | Summary: "Wild—an unusually
    intelligent dog—must stop adorably cute, but dangerous, puppies from being
    released to the public with the help of her friends"— Provided by publisher.
Identifiers: LCCN 2020040884 | ISBN 9780759556218 (hardcover) | ISBN
    9780759556225 (ebook) | ISBN 9780759553910 (ebook other)
Subjects: CYAC: Dogs—Fiction. | Animals—Infancy—Fiction. | Adventure and
    adventurers—Fiction. | Science fiction.
Classification: LCC PZ7.Z21 Pup 2021 | DDC [Fic]—dc23
LC record available at https://lccn.loc.gov/2020040884

ISBNs: 978-0-7595-5620-1 (pbk.), 978-0-7595-5622-5 (ebook)

Printed in the United States of America

LSC-C

Printing 1, 2022

33614082855809

"WHO DO YOU BELONG TO?"

A woman hovers over me, a worried expression on her face. She reaches for my collar to check for a tag, and I instinctively bark and pull away. I left my family on the other side of the park so I could sniff around for some food, and I don't need a stranger cramping my style.

"Don't you know you're not supposed to pet a strange dog?" I ask. "I might take it the wrong way and use your arm as a chew toy."

"How cute," she says. "When you bark, it sounds like you're talking."

"If you only knew," I say, but of course she doesn't know. How could she?

To her I'm just a dog she's come across in the park. She doesn't know I can understand every word she says, much less speak like a human. She'd need a translator earbud to hear me talking, and I have no intention of giving her one. I don't want her to know who I am.

1

I don't want anyone to know.

Today is the dog parade in Lake Balboa Park, and local families have come out to have some fun, bringing their favorite pets with them. I look at the dozens of dogs in costumes. There's a pit bull in a Dodgers baseball uniform, a pug dressed like a fat avocado, and a beagle in an old detective outfit with a sign on his back that says SHERLOCK BONES.

"Why aren't you wearing a costume?" she asks, talking in that baby talk humans often use when they speak to dogs.

"Because I have self-respect," I say.

"You're wearing a collar, so you must have an owner," she says curiously, looking at my neck. "Let's get you to the lost and found."

She reaches to get ahold of me—

"Nice try," I say, darting through her legs and hurrying deeper into the park.

"Is anyone missing a dog?!" I hear her calling behind me, but her shouts are drowned out by the loud music blaring around us.

Besides, I'm not lost. I'm just taking a walk and getting a little me time.

I pass through the dense crowd of people and animals around me. My nose alerts me to something delicious nearby. There's a large booth where people in matching blue T-shirts are handing out dog treats and people treats. I head for the booth, determined to try them both.

There's a high-tech digital sign above the booth:

PUPPIO. THE DOGS OF THE FUTURE.

I've never heard of Puppio. I watch as the screen flashes pictures of incredibly cute puppies with big heads and huge eyes. They look strange, like no breed I've ever seen before. Something about the puppies makes me uneasy.

Maybe it's because they look so happy. It's been a long time since I felt like that.

"What's Puppio?" a man is asking at the booth. An energetic young employee in a blue T-shirt pulls an iPad from his backpack.

"They are the most incredible dogs you'll ever meet," the Puppio employee says, but then a rock band starts playing and drowns out the rest of the conversation.

My instinct is warning me to stay away from the Puppio booth, which is not easy when the treats smell so delicious. I'm torn for a moment, and then I decide to trust my instinct. It's never led me astray before.

I give up on the treats and move toward the music area instead. People are dropping food all over the place, so it shouldn't take me long to find a snack.

I weave around the legs of humans dancing with their dogs, grabbing their front paws while the dogs hop awkwardly on rear legs.

The people seem happy, and the dogs bark like they're having fun. They don't realize they're wearing silly costumes or that people are laughing at them. They don't really understand what's happening; they just know they're fed, happy, and loved.

I wish I could be like them.

"There you are!" a woman says. "The girls are worried. We need to get to the party, Cookie."

3

She calls me Cookie even though that's not my real name. It's the name her girls gave me. I've grown accustomed to answering to it, even though I'm not really a "Cookie" kind of girl. I love a cookie as much as the next dog, but I find the name a little insulting.

I move toward her, letting her get two fingers under my collar so she can attach a leash.

This is the mother of the family I live with now. Her hair is combed straight and dyed blond. She takes herself to the salon every week—I only get groomed once a month.

She and her daughters found me at a dog adoption event a few months ago, and they took me home as their new pet. They didn't know I had snuck into the event, looking for a family and a place where I could hide for a while.

They brought me into their lives, but they have no idea who I am or what I can do. It's safer for everyone that way. I act like a so-called normal dog and I live a normal life. But the truth is I'm hiding from Maelstrom, the organization that created me. I haven't seen any sign of them in over a year, but I know they're hunting me, determined to get me back or end my life.

I'm not sure which they'd prefer, and I don't plan to find out.

"What happened to your costume?" Mom asks as she hustles me through the park.

"The J.K. Howling costume? I tried to wear it, but it didn't fit right," I say, but she's not really speaking to me or listening. She's lost in her own world like she often is, stressed from work and overwhelmed at being the mom of two young teens. I know it's a tough job, but why get a dog if you don't have time to take care of her?

She jogs with me to the parking lot where the girls wait by the car. "I found her," the mom says, but the kids are busy on their phones, and they barely look up.

"Hurry, Mom," the older girl says. "We're going to be late for the party."

We pile into the minivan, and the girls give me a couple quick pats on the head before scooting me into the back so I'm out of the way. I put my head on the seat, hoping for a little scratch behind my ears, but they put on headphones and turn up their music, ignoring me.

I remember when they first brought me home. They couldn't stop giving me attention. Petting, stroking, long walks, treats every day.

That lasted all of a month. Then I was like a piece of furniture, forgotten in the background.

"Belts on," Mom says, "and we are out of here."

"Finally," the older girl says.

Mom presses the ignition button on the van, but nothing happens. "That's strange," she says. She checks to make sure she has her key and presses the ignition button. Again, there's nothing. "I think there's a problem with the engine."

I look up, curious.

"Mom, let's move it," the younger girl says urgently.

"I don't know what to do," Mom says. "Maybe I should get an Uber and I'll have your father call Triple A."

I sit up, sniffing the air. I smell the familiar scents of the car—the girls, the fruit shampoo they use on their hair,

Mom's gym bag, the wrapper from a chocolate bar that fell under the seat and nobody has found in two weeks.

A dozen smells, all of them familiar and neatly categorized in my head.

But then I detect something else. The smallest hint of a man with oil on his fingers.

Did someone touch this car while we were in the park?

A horn beeps behind us. There's an SUV idling, waiting to get into the space. Mom rolls down her window and waves them away.

"You can't park here," she shouts. "My car won't start."

Another beep.

"Geez, that guy's pushy," she says. She steps out of the van.

I watch as Mom approaches a black SUV. A man in a suit waits calmly, his window down.

"You need an Uber?" he asks with a thick Eastern European accent.

"What a coincidence," Mom says. "I was just going to call—"

"No call. I'm your Uber," he says.

"Perfect timing," Mom says with a shrug and hustles back to the van. She opens the door and sticks her head in. "Good news. We're going to the party!"

I look at the Uber, and I feel the fur on the back of my neck rise. There's a large scratch on the front bumper, just like the SUV that cut us off on the way to the park. Is it possible this Uber has been following us?

Mom doesn't seem to notice, and she isn't concerned that

an Uber appeared without even opening the app. She rushes the girls into the SUV, then she comes back for me.

I bark, trying to warn her of my suspicions.

"Not now, Cookie," she says, frustrated. She grabs my leash, ignoring my resistance. She piles into the back seat of the SUV, pulling me in behind her and closing the door.

THE HOUSES ALL
LOOK THE SAME.

Mom stares out the window at a row of expensive gated homes, each with a manicured lawn and large U-shaped driveway.

"I can't remember which house it is," she says.

"It's the white one," her older daughter says.

"They're all white," Mom says, and the Uber driver chuckles.

"The one with all the kids, Mom. Duh." She points and the driver pulls in behind a row of cars dropping off kids for a party.

"I'll take the girls in and I'll be right back," Mom says to the driver. She gets out of the car, and I start to follow. "Wait here, Cookie." She holds up an arm to keep me back.

I bark in protest and nudge forward.

"Too many kids around," Mom says. "I don't want you to get overexcited."

"Right, we wouldn't want a dog to get excited. She might enjoy herself," I say.

Mom ignores my whining, and she shuts the door in my face. I sit back, exasperated.

The sun hits the glass, and I see my reflection in the window looking back at me. My coat is clean and pretty because of occasional trips to the groomer, but I have trouble recognizing myself in the window. Something about this family and this life—it just doesn't feel like me.

"You don't belong here," the Uber driver says.

I think he must be talking on the phone, but when I look up, he's staring at me.

"You're special," he says. "One of a kind."

He's talking to me like he knows I can understand. I recognize his accent now. It's Russian. I shuffle nervously and look out the window, hoping Mom is on her way back.

The driver reaches for something in the glove compartment. The sudden movement puts me on edge, and I clear my throat, letting the rumble fill the car.

"Don't be afraid, beauty," he says.

I bark, warning him to back off. My body tenses as I look for ways out of the SUV. But my instincts are slow, not at all like they were a year ago when I was used to running and fighting as a dog soldier.

I glance out the window again, hoping to see Mom, but she's still in the house. I turn back, ready to defend myself. The driver is holding up what looks like a small aerosol can.

I open my mouth to bite him, but his finger is already

pressing the button on the can, and a cold vapor sprays directly into my face.

I rear back, stunned, and my paws go numb.

I try to reach for the door handle, but the inside of the SUV spins in my vision, and I can't seem to find the handle.

A wave of dizziness hits me, and I stumble and lose my footing.

"Have you been following us?" I try to ask, but the words stick in my throat.

"You don't belong here," he says again.

Where do I belong?

Another burst of spray hits me, and the world goes black.

I DREAM OF THE PAST.

I'm running in a park, wind in my fur as I chase a ball and snatch it from the moist grass.

"Wild! Bring it here!"

It's Chance, the boy I love, the boy who saved my life and whose life I saved in return. In the dream he looks just like I remember him, thick hair falling across his eyes and a wide smile on his face.

He opens his arms to welcome me, and I trot toward him, ball firmly clamped in my teeth. I can detect the oil from his fingers on the ball, a familiar taste and smell that my head defines as "home."

"Thatta girl," Chance says.

I drop the ball into his hands, thrilled to make him happy. He shoves the ball into his pocket and reaches for me, scratching behind my ears. I joyfully wag my tail.

"Is that her?" someone asks loudly.

A man's voice. Thick Russian accent.

My eyes snap open and the dream disappears, replaced by a frightening new reality.

I'm in a wire cage, surrounded by large black crates with locks on them. The walls of the room appear to be made of metal, like some kind of warehouse or storage facility.

How did I get here?

I think back to the Uber with the scratched bumper and the high-tech knockout mist sprayed in my face, and I look at the reinforced steel cage around me—

This is Maelstrom!

That's my first thought. Maelstrom has reappeared after a year, catching me unaware, drugging and capturing me. My muscles tense, my body screaming for me to flee or fight, but I resist both.

I breathe slowly and calm myself. I need more information before I can take action, or I might make the situation worse.

I reach up with a paw and check for my collar.

It's still there.

I sigh with relief. I can understand human language, but I need the collar to translate my barking so humans can understand me. Without it, I have no way of communicating with people.

I hear voices and I tilt my head to the side, moving slowly so whoever it is won't know I'm awake. I peer through half-closed eyes at the three men standing nearby. I recognize one of them as the Uber driver, but he's wearing green coveralls now instead of the business suit he was in earlier. He's next to a big man and a skinny man, all dressed alike.

"How do we know it's her?" the skinny man asks. He has the same accent as the Uber driver, but it's much lighter, like he's been speaking English longer.

"I tested her DNA," the Uber driver says. He pulls out a small electronic device smaller than a cell phone. The skinny man takes it from his hands and presses a button. I see the glow of a screen lighting up.

The skinny man checks the readout, then grunts and slips the device into his pocket. He turns toward me. "She looks like a normal dog."

"There's nothing normal about her," the Uber driver says.

The third man, a big guy with huge shoulders, peers at me. "She doesn't scare me."

"A tiger isn't scary when it's in a cage. But open the door—"

"Whatever," the big man says. "The important thing is we got her before they did."

They zip their coveralls closed, preparing for something. I keep my body limp, hoping they'll be dumb enough to unlock the cage and check on me.

But they don't.

The skinny man stands at a distance, studying me. "Everyone is looking for this dog," he says.

"That's what war is all about," the big man says in Russian. "Everyone wants the same thing, and they're willing to fight to get it."

What war is he talking about? And why is he speaking Russian?

General Rupani and Maelstrom were constantly changing

tactics, but they didn't have Russian accents. Is this a new branch of Maelstrom that's trying to capture me?

The big man touches his ear, and I see he's wearing a radio transmitter of some kind. I hear the squawk of a voice speaking to him.

"Roger that," he says. "Time to move out."

"What about the boy?" the big man asks.

My body tenses, my breathing quick and shallow.

"We haven't located the boy yet," the Uber driver says, "but we'll have him by tonight."

They're talking about Chance.

"What will you do with him?" the man asks.

"We'll hang on to him. He's our insurance policy if the dog gets uncooperative."

My heart leaps as I think of him. I haven't seen Chance in over a year. I remember the last time we were together. Chance begged me to stay with him and his mother, but I had to leave. With Maelstrom hunting me, he wouldn't be safe if I stuck around.

Now it seems Maelstrom has caught up with me and staying away from Chance hasn't worked. He's in as much danger as I am.

"We need to hurry," the skinny man says, and he motions for the others to get moving.

The Uber driver comes toward my cage, removing a small aerosol can from his pocket.

It's the knockout spray.

I squint so it looks like I'm still asleep.

"What's with the spray?" the skinny man asks.

"An extra dose, just to make sure she doesn't wake up."

The Uber driver leans over the cage. "Have a nice sleep, doggy," he says, and he sprays the wet mist in my face.

This time I'm ready for it, and I close my eyes tight and hold my breath. The vapor hits me, but I don't breathe it in. I moan and go limp at the bottom of the cage, pretending to fall even more deeply asleep.

I lie there quietly, unmoving, listening as the men file out of the room and close the door behind them.

When they're gone, I shake my head violently, flapping my ears to get the chemical mist away from me. I open my eyes and take a deep breath, fully alert.

Now I have to figure a way out of the cage.

Before I can make a move, I hear the rumble of engines starting, and the floor vibrates and starts to move. I leap up on all fours, my senses on fire.

The engine roar increases until it's deafening. I sniff the air, my nose categorizing a hundred different scents at one time. I smell my fur, the scent of the men who were here, the electronics stored in the black cases around me, and something else, a sulfur odor that is growing stronger with every second.

Jet fuel.

That's when I realize—this room isn't a warehouse.

It's the cargo hold of an airplane.

And the plane is taking off....

I SLAM MYSELF AGAINST THE SIDE OF THE CAGE.

The wire frame bends but doesn't break. The plane accelerates beneath me, the tires rumbling down the runway.

I swallow hard, fighting the panic growing inside. I back up as much as possible, and I fling myself into the side of the cage again. The wire bends more but remains intact. I glance across the cargo hold at the door on the far side, half expecting the men to come running in, but they can't hear me over the noise of the engines.

I can see the indentation of my body in the cage wire. One more time should do the trick.

Suddenly, the plane lifts into the air, and I stumble back as the nose points skyward. I hear the mechanical whir of the landing gear retracting into the belly of the plane.

I have to get out of here. Now.

I gather myself and hit the side of the cage with all my strength. The frame bursts, spilling me onto the floor.

I'm free!

I race toward the cabin door, ducking my head at the last moment and hitting it with my body. The door pops open, and I roll several times, coming up on all fours, ready for anything.

The men are strapped into their seats. Three heads turn simultaneously as I'm met with stunned looks and Russian curses.

"She escaped!" one of them screams.

"Get her!" the Uber driver shouts.

They reach for their belts, struggling to free themselves.

I've only got seconds. I scan the cabin, looking for an escape. This doesn't look like the photos of planes I've seen before. It's an open space with a dozen seats bolted to the sides with green webbing between them.

Is this a military plane?

There's a red Exit sign over the door in the front of the cabin. That's my way out.

The men are rising from their seats now. They make their way down the aisle, fighting to keep their balance as they approach.

"This is not my idea of a vacation," I say, and I run at full speed up the aisle, zigzagging to avoid their outstretched hands.

I get to the exit door, which is sealed with a lever arm across the center, and I reach for the lever with my mouth—

"Don't do it!" the Uber driver shouts behind me, but he's too late.

I grab the door lever and pull up.

A red light flashes, a buzzer goes off, and the door instantly snaps open.

A violent wind fills the cabin with a roar so loud it makes my ears ache. I glance out the door and catch sight of the ground far below. The houses look like children's toys.

I underestimated the speed of the plane. We're already several thousand feet in the air.

"There's nowhere to go, dog," the Uber driver says. He has to shout to be heard over the noise in the cabin.

I turn and plant my feet, fur buffeted by the screaming wind.

"I know you can understand what I'm saying," he shouts. "We're not going to hurt you."

"Then why did you lock me in a cage?" I ask.

He cocks his head, curious. "I know we can't speak to each other directly, but I meant what I said earlier. You're special, and we have a special place for you. Give us a chance to explain."

I look from one man to the other. *Can I trust these guys?*

I want to believe them, but I think about how they drugged me and locked me up. The way they're talking about kidnapping Chance.

That snaps me back to reality.

The skinny man comes toward me, reaching to grab my neck. I crouch down and bark at full volume with teeth bared, warning him to stay away.

"Good doggy," he says, and he pulls out a can of knock-out spray.

"That won't work in the wind," the Uber driver shouts at him.

The driver grabs a pole off the wall and passes it to the skinny guy. One end has a loop to capture me around my neck. He flips a button, and I hear the crackle of electricity surging through the pole.

"Stun her!" the driver shouts, and he grabs his own pole from the wall. They come toward me, poles outstretched, the air in front of them crackling with ozone.

"Give up, dog!" the Uber driver shouts.

I look frantically for a way out of this mess.

Three men in front of me, two of them with weapons. The open sky behind me with a several-thousand-foot drop.

Maybe the driver is right. I'm out of options.

I glance to my side and see the skinny man strapping on a large backpack.

A parachute.

The plane banks hard, and the angle in the cabin shifts, knocking the men off their feet. They go down in a tumble, poles clattering to the ground.

I seize the opportunity to dart toward the skinny man, avoiding his attempt to kick me by biting down on his arm.

He howls in pain and tries to get away from me, but I clamp harder and tug him toward the open door of the plane.

"No, no, no!" he shouts as I pull him a few inches at a time.

The other men try to grab their poles and get to their feet, but they're far away across the cabin now, and they can't move fast enough.

"Help me!" he shouts to them.

I drag him farther, my rear paws at the very edge of the open door. He blinks in astonishment as he realizes how strong I am. I may look like a normal dog, but I'm more powerful than a whole pack of dogs put together.

"What's she doing?!" he shouts, terrified.

"That's for me to know and you to find out," I mumble through closed jaws.

With a final burst of effort, I pull him the rest of the way across the cabin and out the door. A second later we're falling into open air, my jaws firmly attached to the skinny man's arm.

WE TUMBLE THROUGH THE SKY.

The skinny man screams in terror and curses wildly. They're the kinds of words people usually don't say in public, but when you're hurtling through the air at 120 miles per hour with a dog's teeth clamped on your arm, I guess you say whatever comes to mind.

I look down and see the cars and trees growing in size with every second that passes. I don't know exactly how high we were when we left the plane, but I'm guessing we've got less than a minute to free-fall before the parachute has to open.

Time to take action. The skinny man is still screaming and thrashing under me. He's trying to reach for the rip cord that opens the parachute, but I've got one of his arms in my teeth and my body is blocking the other arm. If he's going to open the parachute, I have to get out of the way.

But to do that, I'm going to have to let go.

I feel the wind and judge the rotation of our bodies in the air. Then I unlatch from his arm.

He immediately reaches for the rip cord as I fall away from him. His fingers close around the cord...and I twist in the air and bite down on his calf. He screams and pulls the cord at the same time.

The chute opens and we're yanked upward, the man howling while I hang on to his leg for dear life. A minute later we're drifting slowly toward the ground. I see the tall buildings of downtown Los Angeles to the south and the Verdugo Mountains to the north. The man seems to know where we are, and he pulls hard at the steering lines, aiming for a large patch of green far below.

With the immediate danger gone, the man turns his attention to me. He kicks at me with his free foot, desperate to knock me off. His foot makes contact with my head.

Wrong move, buddy.

I crane my neck muscles and pull my body up his leg, gaining a paw hold on his pants and climbing his body an inch at a time. His eyes grow wide as he sees me getting closer to his face.

The whole thing is too much for him, and he screams and passes out. I feel his body go limp and I climb the rest of the way, digging my teeth into the fabric around his chest and hanging on tight for the short ride to the ground.

His eyes open just before we hit. He sees me hanging on to his chest, screams, and passes out again.

We land hard—him first on his back, and me on his chest.

I hop off and stand in the cool grass. I pause to catch my breath. After the roar of wind in my ears, being on the ground is strangely silent.

I think about the events of the last few hours. The minivan that wouldn't start, the Uber driver who appeared out of nowhere, the knockout spray, and the strange Maelstrom agents who speak Russian.

Who are these guys and where were they taking me?

I look up and see the plane far in the distance. It's making a long, slow turn in the sky, banking back toward the airport where we must have taken off.

This is not over. In fact, it's only the beginning.

I look to the skinny man on the ground.

"Hey, buddy," I say, but he doesn't move.

I sniff at his neck. He's alive and breathing, but it looks like he's going to be out for a while.

I have to figure out where I am. I look at the expanse of trees and breathe deeply, catching a scent of wild animals nearby.

The Griffith Park Zoo.

I take a step and my paw bumps into something. It's the small electronic device the Uber driver was holding when he talked about checking my DNA. It must have gotten dislodged from the skinny man's pocket when we hit the ground.

The device is off, the screen black.

I roll over and use a paw to slip the device between my neck and collar. I may need it later to figure out who the Russians are.

I think about what I overheard on the plane when I first woke up. The Russians said everyone is looking for me, and they mentioned some kind of war. All of that worries me, but not as much as what the Uber driver said.

We haven't located the boy yet, but we'll have him by tonight.

Chance is in trouble.

I check the Russian man's watch. It's two in the afternoon. I haven't seen Chance in over a year, but I memorized the address of his new apartment and school a long time ago.

Now I have to get to him before Maelstrom does.

I HEAR CHILDREN
SCREAM.

I've been running for an hour before I approach Chance's school, my heart thumping in my chest. The children scream again followed by a loud whistle and the sound of people clapping.

What's going on?

I turn the corner and see a soccer game in progress on the field behind Chance's school.

It's just a game, girl.

I slow down, my breathing returning to normal. I smell Chance before I see him, his scent familiar to me even though it's intermingled with the scents of dozens of kids on the field.

I scan the players, searching for his face. One player weaves his way through a group of kids trying to get to the ball.

It's Chance!

He's grown since I last saw him. His jaw has thickened a little, and his face is more mature than I remember. But there's no question it's him. A shiver of joy passes through me from snout to tail, and I take off, racing onto the field, ignoring the surprised looks of the bystanders and shouts for me to stop.

I dart into the middle of the action, running through players' legs as I sprint toward Chance. A player kicks the ball and it whizzes toward me. I pivot and easily kick it away with my rear legs.

"Nice move," a player says, then he realizes what just happened. "Hey, there's a dog out here!"

Chaos erupts on the field, the spectators shouting and the players reaching for me. They think I'm a stray dog that has wandered onto the field, and a few of them reach for my collar.

I turn this way and that, dodging their outstretched arms as I make my way toward Chance.

I instantly cover the distance between us. I stop at his feet, barking and looking up at him.

He stares at me, confused.

"Is that your dog?" the referee shouts at him.

"It's not my—" Chance stops midsentence, examining me more closely. He looks at my special collar, the same one I wore when he last saw me over a year ago.

His mouth drops open in astonishment. "Wild? Is that you?"

I bark and rub my head against his bare leg.

"Where did you come from?" he says in disbelief.

"I can explain everything," I say. I know he can't understand me yet, so I plead with my eyes and motion toward the sidelines with my snout.

"It is his dog!" a player says.

"Get the dog off the field!" the opposing coach shouts.

"Penalty card!" another player shouts.

"I don't think we have a penalty for a dog on the field," the confused referee says.

"She's not my dog," Chance says.

The words sting, and my breathing quickens.

"Sorry about this," Chance says to the players. "I'll take care of her."

He slips a finger under my collar and pulls me toward the sidelines.

"What are you doing here?" he whispers under his breath as he speeds up, guiding me off the field and around the corner of the school building where we can't be seen.

"I can't believe it's you," he says. "Why would you run into the middle of the field during a game? Why would you come here at all?"

He runs his fingers through his hair in surprise and confusion.

I bark and turn my head, exposing my collar to him. He hesitates, and I nudge his hand with my muzzle, urging him toward the collar.

"Your nose is wet," he says, and he wipes his hand on his shorts.

I move closer to him and concentrate hard. The secret compartment on the back of my collar opens, revealing the earbud that will allow us to communicate with each other.

Chance hesitates. I'm afraid he's not going to take it. Then he sighs and reaches down to remove the tiny earbud from my collar.

He holds the bud in his palm, considering it—

I bark, and he gives in. He pinches the bud in his fingers and puts it in his ear. He squints as the pain hits and the bud connects to his auditory nerve. He once told me the sensation was like a tiny lightning bolt striking his ear.

"Can you understand me now?" I ask.

He gasps. "I haven't heard your voice in a long time," he says.

I wag my tail joyously, and his energy softens. "I thought you were gone forever."

A whistle blows around the corner, and I hear the shouts of players as the game starts up again.

"How did you even know where to find me?" Chance asks.

"I've been keeping track of you from far away. I memorized your address, your new school's location, everything about you."

"You knew where I was all this time, and you never came to visit me?"

He tries to hide it, but I can see the hurt on his face.

"I wanted to see you every day," I say. "But I couldn't."

"Why not?"

"Because of Maelstrom."

He shivers when he hears the name.

"That's why I came today. Maelstrom is back."

"That's impossible," he says.

"There was an Uber driver with knockout spray. Then I was on a plane and they had—"

"Whoa, slow down," Chance says. "I can barely follow you."

I stop, realizing how strange this must sound to him. A dog he hasn't seen in a year runs into the middle of his soccer game shouting about bad guys.

"I can explain everything later," I say. "But right now we have to get out of here. You're in danger."

"What kind of danger?"

"These Maelstrom guys with Russian accents are coming."

"Maelstrom didn't have Russian accents."

"Maybe they're a new branch or—"

A whistle blows, and I hear footsteps running toward us.

"Chance Anderson! Where are you?"

"I'm here, Coach!" Chance shouts. He whispers urgently, "Don't say anything, Wild. Pretend you're a regular dog."

Chance's coach runs around the corner and comes toward us.

"What are you doing in the parking lot with a dog?" Coach asks.

"It's my neighbor's dog," Chance says. "She must have run away."

"We're in the middle of a game, son. You can play with the mutt later."

I growl, not liking the way this guy talks about dogs. Chance puts a hand on my shoulder, calming me.

"I'm sorry, Coach. I'll be right back," Chance says.

"Tie her up and get back on the field. Your team needs you." The coach blows his whistle one last time and jogs away.

"I hope he swallows that whistle," I say.

I'm expecting Chance to laugh, but when I look up, his cheeks are red with embarrassment.

"This is a new school for me," he says. "I'm trying to make a good impression."

"I just—"

"Now I'm in trouble. Thanks for nothing, Wild."

I whimper and lower my head. "I'm really sorry. But you're going to be in bigger trouble if we don't get out of here."

"I can't leave. I'm in the middle of a game."

"Didn't you hear me a minute ago? Maelstrom is coming!"

The crowd cheers wildly at the game. Chance hesitates, looking from the field to me.

"I have to get back," Chance says. "I'm happy to see you. Really, I am. You just freaked me out a little when you ran onto the field."

He reaches to take out the earbud.

"Wait, Chance!"

But he doesn't wait. He takes it out, touches my collar to open the compartment, and replaces the bud.

I bark repeatedly, urging him to put the earbud back in so we can talk.

"I'm sorry, girl. Come to the apartment tonight. We'll figure it out then."

I whimper and nip at his shorts leg, begging him to talk to me again.

"I'm sorry. I have to go." He jogs away, waving to me once before disappearing around the corner.

I howl in pain and frustration, falling back on my hind legs, tail slapping the asphalt.

"Where's your owner?" a woman asks.

I turn and see a teacher walking to her car with a heavy box of school supplies in her hands. My crying must have caught her attention.

I can tell she wants to reach for me, but her hands are full. I skitter away and duck between cars.

"Hey, wait!" she says. But I'm already out of sight and out of reach. I hear her sigh and keep walking.

"Oh, well," she says. "You can't save them all."

I think about my options. I'm not going to run onto the field and embarrass Chance again, but I can't leave him alone either.

I have to find a hiding place where I can watch for danger until Chance is done with the game and I can talk to him again.

I scan the parking lot until I find the right spot—a maintenance shed in the far corner with the door partly open. I make a run for it, determined to keep Chance safe no matter what.

CHILDREN'S SCREAMS SNAP ME AWAKE.

The light is fading, and I realize I must have drifted off from exhaustion. I race to the doors of the utility shed and peer through the crack.

The soccer game has just ended, and the kids and parents are streaming into the parking lot, laughing and bragging as they recount the events of the game.

I spot Chance in the crowd. He's walking with a fellow player and his parents. I scan the parking lot for any sign of Maelstrom, but I don't see anything that makes me suspicious. Chance's friend offers him a ride and they get into a Honda with his parents.

I wonder where Chance's mom is. Why wasn't she at the game to see him play?

I don't have time to think about it right now because the Honda pulls out, and I follow the headlights, determined to keep Chance in sight until he gets home safely.

I start at a trot, picking up speed as the car accelerates. I don't want to be spotted, so I stay off to the side, dashing down the sidewalk, hopping over bushes, and running across lawns.

The car starts to get away from me, so I leap from the ground to an orange tree, scurrying up through the branches until I reach the highest point. Then I jump across open air and land on the terra-cotta rooftop of a nearby house.

I jump from one roof to the next, keeping the car in view, chasing without being seen.

I'm extra careful up there, testing my balance and making sure to move as silently as possible. If the homeowners hear anything, they'll think it's a raccoon. Nobody would expect a dog to be running across their roof.

It takes about ten minutes for the car to arrive at its destination, a run-down apartment complex in West LA where Chance gets out.

I watch from the roof of a house across the street as Chance waves to his friend, then heads to the second floor. I look at the name of the apartment complex and recognize it from my research. This is the place Chance and his mother moved to a few months ago.

There's a bright billboard illuminating the sky above me. A smiling puppy looking down at me from thirty feet in the air.

PUPPIO. THE DOGS OF THE FUTURE.
COMING SOON TO SANTA MONICA AND BEYOND.

It's that company again, the same one that had a booth at the costume parade in the park. I stare at the cute puppy on the billboard, its eyes wide with innocence.

Was I ever a puppy like that?

Snap out of it, girl.

I shake off the distraction. I have to talk to Chance and convince him he's in danger. I leap off the roof and head for his apartment.

I SCRATCH AT THE LIVING ROOM WINDOW WITH MY PAW.

Chance hears the noise and stands up to investigate. He gasps when he sees me and breaks into a smile. He points toward the front door. I check to make sure nobody is in the hall outside the apartment, and I trot to the door and slip inside.

We look at each other, truly alone for the first time. Chance drops to his knees and reaches for me, capturing me in a bear hug. I squirm and whine, tail beating a loud pattern on the linoleum. I'm overcome with emotion at seeing him. Everything about him is familiar except his scent. It takes me a while to understand what's changed.

Chance doesn't smell like a boy anymore.

He smells like a young man.

"You must be worried about me, girl. You followed me all the way home."

I bark and nod my head, and he reaches for my collar to

release the earbud. He frowns as he adjusts to the discomfort, and then his face relaxes.

"Can you hear me?" I ask.

"Loud and clear, Wild. It's good to hear your voice again. Sorry I yelled at you earlier."

"You must have been surprised to see me."

"That's the understatement of the year."

"You're in danger."

"That stuff you were saying about Maelstrom earlier."

"That's right."

"It's impossible," Chance says. "Maelstrom's gone."

"What do you mean gone?"

"They don't exist anymore."

"How do you know?" I ask.

"Junebug told me."

I yelp involuntarily. "You talked to Junebug?"

"We met up a few months ago," Chance says. "She lives with her aunt in Brentwood now."

"It's dangerous to talk to her!" I say.

Junebug's father is General Rupani, the founder of Maelstrom. She may have helped us to battle him once, but she's still his flesh and blood.

"It's not dangerous," Chance says. "We defeated General Rupani, and I haven't seen Maelstrom since then. Junebug said she hasn't heard from her father either. Nobody in the family has."

"That's why you looked at me funny when I mentioned Maelstrom back at the field."

He nods. "They can't be back because they don't exist."

I think about the Russians who attacked me. The knock-out spray. The electric capture nooses.

"Something exists," I say. "I was captured earlier. I'm not making that up."

Chance looks baffled, but before he can ask me what's going on, I hear a key in the lock.

The door swings open and his mother walks in carrying a big bag from California Chicken Cafe. I can smell the delicious odor wafting through the apartment.

I remember his mom from last year when I met her at the treatment center. She looks healthier. She's gained a little weight, and she has the same messy brown hair as Chance. She obviously doesn't remember me because she jumps and lets out a little scream when she sees me.

"What is that thing?" she asks.

"It's not a thing. It's a dog," Chance says.

"What's it doing in our apartment?"

"Not it. *She*. Use the right pronoun, Mom."

"Tell her you're watching me for a friend," I say to Chance.

Chance's mom hears me barking, but she can't understand what I'm saying.

"Keep her quiet, Chance! The neighbors will hear. Now tell me what she's doing here."

Chance speaks fast. "A guy on the team. His house is being fumigated and he needed a place for her to stay since they couldn't take her to a hotel."

"We've discussed this before, and we can't have dogs," Mom says. "The landlord won't allow it."

"But she has no place to go."

"Neither do we if we get thrown out of here."

"Please, Mom."

I give her my best "friendly dog" look—tongue lolling out, heavy breathing, tail swinging. Humans love that kind of thing.

Chance clasps his hands together in front of his chin, pleading. "Just one night."

His mom sighs. "One night. No noise. Nobody can know there's a dog in this building."

Chance smiles. "I promise she won't even bark once."

"How are you going to keep a dog from barking?"

"She's a very smart dog," Chance says, and he throws me a wink.

Mom shakes her head. "I hope I don't regret this." She puts the bag of chicken down on the kitchen table and hurries to her bedroom. "I'm going to change real quick, then I have to get to my AA meeting."

"What's new," Chance mutters under his breath.

His mom stops and her face turns red. I can see she's angry, and she struggles to keep her voice even.

"You can come with me if you want," his mom says.

"I don't feel comfortable at meetings."

His mom sighs, frustrated. Then she looks at the clock. "Enjoy your dinner. Just remember to put the leftovers in the refrigerator."

"There won't be any leftovers," I say, and I lick my lips.

Chance shushes me as his mom rushes out of the room.

"Welcome to the new normal," he says. "She stops by the house for three seconds between work and twelve-step meetings, just long enough to make sure I don't die of starvation and I'm doing my homework."

"That kind of sucks," I say.

"No kidding. That's why she wasn't at the game. She's only seen me play once. Can you believe it?"

"It sounds like she's doing her best."

"Whose side are you on?" Chance asks, and he slumps down at the table and opens the bag of food.

He takes out rotisserie chicken, potatoes, and some kind of cabbage salad. Mom hurries back through the kitchen. She kisses Chance on the forehead, grabs a chicken leg, then runs for the door. "I'll be back in two hours max," she says, and she's gone.

Chance sighs and looks at the food.

"Are you as hungry as I am?" I ask.

The smell of roast chicken is hypnotic. My stomach rumbles, reminding me I haven't eaten all day. I need to walk around the apartment, secure the perimeter, make sure we're safe from any threats. But I'm not going to be able to do any of that without some food in my belly.

"Let's eat," Chance says, "and you can tell me what happened earlier."

I dig into a chunk of chicken, and I start to tell my story.

"WHERE DID YOU GET THIS?" CHANCE ASKS.

We're sitting in Chance's bedroom after dinner. He's staring at the DNA device I took from the skinny Russian's pocket after we fell from the plane.

"I told you. The Maelstrom soldier."

He turns the device over in his hands. "What is it exactly?"

"I overheard them saying they used it to read my DNA."

"Why would they need your DNA?"

"To identify me. They wanted to make sure they had the right dog. And they mentioned a boy."

"It sounds strange, Wild. Are you sure they were talking about me?"

I whine in frustration, not knowing what to tell him. They didn't use his name exactly, but what other boy could they have been talking about?

He presses a button on the device, and the screen comes to life. "Whoa, what's happening?" he says.

"Be careful," I say.

He immediately covers the screen with his hand, and a loud tone sounds. A light on the side of the device flashes green.

Chance looks at the screen and gasps.

"What is it?" I ask.

He holds it out to me. The screen says:

Chance Anderson, 99.98% probable match

"You were right," he says, his face pale.

"Turn it off! Fast."

He presses frantically at the button, and the screen goes black again. He drops the device and slumps down in a chair.

"I think Maelstrom is back," I say quietly.

"But you said they were Uber drivers with Russian accents. That doesn't sound like Maelstrom."

"No, it doesn't."

"I heard about these groups that steal dogs. Maybe they were dog thieves?"

"You mean dog and kid thieves. They're looking for the both of us."

Chance bites at his nail, his face lined with worry. "What should we do?" he asks.

I think about our options. We're both exhausted, and it's late.

"I think we should stay here overnight," I say.

"But what about—" He points at the device.

"There are neighbors all around us in the apartment

complex. If those people are still chasing us, they're not going to come here in the middle of the night."

Chance nods, thinking it through. "I guess you're right. And it would be nice to spend some time with you again."

I look around Chance's bedroom, taking in the books on the shelf, the bed with thick pillows, the pile of clothes on the floor that fill the room with his scent.

"I'll stay with you for tonight," I say. "And we'll figure this out in the morning."

"Great," he says with a smile.

"Now I have to get rid of this device." I reach over to scoop it off the desk.

"What will you do with it?"

"I'll take it outside and bury it. And while I'm out there, I need to do my business."

Chance laughs.

"What's so funny?"

"You're so much like a human sometimes, I forget that you don't use the toilet."

"I'm not really into toilets," I say.

"Okay, I'll take you out for a walk."

"I think I'd better go alone. If a neighbor sees me, they won't know where I'm staying, and you won't get in trouble."

I also want to check around the apartment complex, and I can't do that if Chance is with me.

Chance nods. "Tap on the door when you get back and I'll let you in."

"Will do," I say. He opens the front door, checks to make sure nobody is in the hall, and lets me out.

I make my way through the apartment complex to the yard in the back, my nose alert to danger. Nothing strikes me as out of place, so I dig a hole in the soft ground, drop the DNA device into it, and fill it with dirt.

Once it's hidden, I sniff around several trees, delighted at the lack of dog smells. I guess there really aren't any dogs in this apartment complex. I find the best tree and settle in to do my business.

I hear rustling from deep in the woods behind the apartment complex. I freeze, senses at full alert. I peer into the woods, my eyes adjusting to the darkness there.

First there's nothing. Only the sound of wind in the leaves.

Then a set of eyes appear in the distance, glowing red. I jerk back, my muscles tensing in anticipation of a fight.

The red eyes blink out, and I shake my head, unsure if I'm seeing things. I scan the trees, hoping I've imagined it.

The eyes appear again, closer this time. They are low to the ground, at the height of an animal's head. The wind shifts toward me, and I sniff deep, but I can't detect any scent.

If there's an animal out there, I should smell it by now.

Unless that animal is able to mask its scent.

Unless it's the Maelstrom dog I fought in the mountains long ago.

The Finisher.

The name sends a chill through my body. The Finisher is a dog with stealth capabilities sent on a mission to kill me.

When I last fought him, he plunged over the edge of a cliff and disappeared into the mist below.

No animal should be able to survive a fall like that. No *normal* animal.

But the Finisher is not normal. He's a hybrid dog like I am. He was created before me with a different generation of Maelstrom breeding and a different skill set.

As I stare into the forest now, my instinct tells me the Finisher is alive and well, and he's come back for me.

I creep forward, belly to the ground, readying myself for an attack. I won't be able to smell the Finisher, but his eyes will give him away. If I can follow them, I may have a split second to prepare before the attack comes.

I stay locked on his eyes. I hold my breath and wait, my fur standing on end.

I hear brakes squeal behind me, and the red glow of the eyes blinks out.

Headlights bounce off the trees as two cars turn into the apartment complex driveway, moving fast.

I look into the forest, but the eyes have disappeared.

I hear doors slam, and I snap to attention. I hear men speaking Russian in the parking lot behind me. I turn away from the trees, forgetting about the Finisher, my mind focused on one thing alone.

I have to get back to Chance.

I RACE BACK TOWARD THE APARTMENT COMPLEX.

I peek around the corner and see three men in dark suits heading toward the front staircase. I don't recognize the men, but their accents are unmistakable.

I race away, shooting up the back stairs so I can get to Chance's apartment before they do.

I turn the corner just as a woman with a laundry basket steps out of her apartment. She freezes when she sees me. "Is that a coyote?" she says. "Ned, I think there's a coyote in the hall!"

"You're obsessed with coyotes!" a gruff man says from inside the house.

I run past her and she screams. I pick up speed, barking and calling out to Chance.

He flings the door open. "Quiet, Wild!"

"We have to go. Now!"

"What are you talking about?"

"The Russians found us—"

But it's too late to say more. The suited men come around the corner, and Chance gasps and pulls me into the apartment, bolting the door.

"Those are the guys you were telling me about," Chance whispers.

"Different guys," I say. "Same accents."

"I shouldn't have turned on the stupid device!" Chance says.

There's a loud knock.

Chance's breathing quickens.

"Is there a back door?" I ask.

"Front door only."

"What about the window?"

"One window leads to the hall where they are, and the back window—well, it's a long way down."

Another knock, louder this time.

"What should we do?" Chance asks.

I calculate the odds of running versus fighting, the possibility of calling the police and trying to hold the men off until they arrive.

All decent plans, but all of them have a high probability of Chance getting injured.

There's more thumping on the door, and I realize there's only one option.

"Let them in," I tell Chance.

"What?!"

"They didn't see me yet, so they don't know I'm here."

"What does that mean?"

"It means we have the element of surprise. They think

they're going to find you alone. Open the door and let them in. When I bark, drop to your knees."

"Is that the whole plan?"

I tilt my head at a funny angle and blink my eyes.

"Are you trying to wink at me?" he asks.

"It's my best imitation."

Chance laughs and I feel the tension drain from his body.

"Okay," he says. "Here goes nothing."

I jump behind the sofa where I can't be seen, and I listen as Chance walks to the door and unlocks it.

"Is your mother at home?" a man asks.

"She's in the other room," Chance lies. "Are you friends of hers?"

"Friends? Um—yeah. Tell her friends are at the door."

"Okay," Chance says. "Wait here."

"We'll wait inside," the man says forcefully.

"No problem at all," Chance says with false bravado. "Any friend of my mom's is a friend of mine."

I hear three sets of footsteps as the men come into the small apartment.

"One second and I'll get my mom," Chance says.

I wait until he's across the room from the men, and I let out a short, staccato bark.

Chance drops to his knees, and I jump up on the couch, taking in the scene in a flash. Chance on all fours, the men in suits looming behind him, startled.

I roar at top volume and leap, soaring over Chance's back. I hit the first man like a bowling ball, sending him careening into his friend, the two of them stumbling into the wall, then falling to the ground. I land and spin in place, instantly jumping toward the third man. I kick him in the throat and he falls, breathless and clutching at his chest.

I open the door with my teeth and turn back to Chance. "Let's go!" I shout, then I unleash a volley of ferocious barking to disorient the men, who are scrambling on the ground, tangled in one another's legs.

Chance runs past them, following me into the hallway and closing the door behind him. "You're amazing!" he shouts.

"We're not safe yet," I say. I rush down the hall, moving toward the red box I saw on the wall earlier.

The fire alarm.

I jump and slam the glass with my paw, pulling the lever and triggering a loud alarm through the apartment complex.

The door of Chance's apartment flies open, and the three men rush out and immediately notice us at the end of the hall.

"Stop!" the first one shouts, and he and his buddies are in motion, coming at us fast. The first guy reaches into his jacket and pulls out a small aerosol can, just like the spray used to knock me out in the Uber.

Chance is stunned at the sight of them, and I have to yank his pant leg to get him moving.

"Run!" I shout, and he does, the two of us sprinting down the hall with a tiny head start.

I glance back to see the men gaining on us. At this pace, they're going to catch us in less than ten seconds. One of them is already reaching forward, ready to grab Chance once he's close enough.

I'm looking for a way to defend us when apartment doors start opening. Neighbors pour into the hall to find out why the fire alarm is going off. The hallway fills up, blocking the men who are chasing us. Their progress slows as they fight their way through the neighbors.

Chance and I run downstairs to the first floor, where we bump into the woman I saw earlier. She looks at Chance, then at me, and she lets out a long, high-pitched wail.

"Ned, the coyote is back!" she shouts.

"She's not a coyote," Chance says, annoyed, and we keep running.

I hear the conversations of the neighbors behind us, some of them asking about the fire and some wondering about the dog they've seen.

Farther up the stairs, I hear a scream followed by angry shouts.

"That's rude!" a man says.

"Stop pushing!" another says.

I glance back and see the source of the commotion. The men in suits are forcing their way through the crowd, pushing people out of the way as they rush down the stairs toward us.

Chance and I run into the parking lot. I look around frantically, trying to figure out our next move.

Chance heads for a large truck and motions for me to follow. We crouch behind it, temporarily hidden from the view of the people in the apartment complex.

I listen to the sounds around us. Neighbors are streaming out into the yard and moving away from the building. Then I hear the click of dress shoes on pavement.

Three sets of dress shoes.

The men in suits haven't given up. They're still looking for us.

"Check over there," one of them says, his accent distinct.

Chance looks at me with fear in his eyes. "I'm sorry I doubted you," he whispers. "And I'm sorry I touched that device."

"It's not your fault," I say. "I'm the one who suggested we stay here." I lick his face, letting him know it's okay.

"We can't stay here now, can we?" he asks.

The footsteps spread out as the men search the parking lot.

Alone, I could easily outrun them. But with Chance?

My ears prick up, alerted by a high-pitched sound carried on the wind.

Sirens. Moving fast.

"The fire trucks will be here soon," I tell Chance.

"I don't hear anything."

The sirens come into the range of human hearing, and Chance's eyebrows rise.

"I forgot how big your ears are," he says.

"When the sirens get close, walk to the first firefighter you see and tell them you're scared. They'll take care of you until the police arrive."

Chance stares at me in the darkness. "You're leaving?"

"I can't stay with you. A lot of your neighbors saw me, and Maelstrom knows I'm here."

"They know I'm here, too. What about me?"

"I don't think they'll do anything now that the authorities are involved. And once the police are here—"

"Remember the police officer that picked us up last year? He was working for Maelstrom."

Chance is right. Maelstrom had infiltrated the police, or at least some of them.

"That was a single officer," I tell Chance. "There's going to be dozens of them here. I'll come back once I'm sure it's safe."

I stand up to leave, and Chance throws his arms around me.

"I'm going with you," he says.

"I can't let you do that," I say.

"You need me, Wild. What's your plan?"

"I'll track these guys to their base, or wherever they're coming from."

"How will you get around? It's not like you can call a cab."

"I'll manage."

"Maybe. But it will be much easier if we do it together."

"It's too dangerous," I say. "And I can't take you away from home. What will your mother say?"

The footsteps approach the truck where we're hiding. I have to make a choice.

Leave Chance here or take him with me?

He's right that it will be easier with him. He can do things I can't do and have conversations I can't have on my own. I'd do anything not to put him in danger, but I can't be sure he's not in danger if he stays here.

I bring my face close to his, breathing in his excitement and fear. "Let's go together," I say.

"For real?"

I nod.

Chance throws his arms around me and captures me in a bear hug. "Thank you!" he says.

A shadow falls over us. "Here they are," a man shouts.

Chance screams and I whirl around to see one of the men in suits coming toward us, a can of knockout spray in his hands.

"Time to go!" I shout to Chance, and I roar and leap at the man, knocking the can from his hands and striking him dead center in the chest. He trips and falls back, hitting his head on the pavement.

Chance and I take off, racing to the edge of the parking lot.

The sirens are louder now. The fire trucks are on their way.

"Which direction?" Chance shouts as we hit the sidewalk.

I look back and see the men racing after us. They'll be here before the fire department will. Do we run back where there are people, or do we risk the street at night?

"Look at that!" Chance shouts.

Two black sedans with Uber placards sit at the edge of the parking lot with engines idling. Evidently the men thought they would snatch us and be gone by now, but we messed up their plans.

"Let's steal one of their cars," Chance says.

"Since when can you drive?" I ask.

"My mom's been letting me practice a little in empty parking lots."

We run toward the cars. Chance jumps in the driver's seat of one, while I hop into the other, press the ignition button to turn it off, then grab the fob from the center console and take it with me.

I get back into Chance's Uber and pull the door closed behind me.

"Back up and let's get out of here," I say.

"I can't go in reverse yet."

I glance in the mirror. The men are rushing toward us, waving their arms and shouting.

"Then do a K-turn and—"

"I'm not good with turns," Chance says.

The men get to the car and start pounding on the trunk.

"Floor it, Chance!"

"I know how to do that!" He slams the gas, and the car lurches forward. We jump the curb and drive up on the lawn, mowing down bushes as we go. I point to the place where a rear driveway leads out of the complex. Chance yanks the wheel to the right, clipping a street sign as he pops back onto pavement and out into the street.

Behind us, the first fire trucks are pulling into the apartment complex. We head down the street in the opposite direction, quickly putting distance between ourselves and the men behind us.

Chance steals a glance in the rearview mirror, then he shouts in joy. "Did you see what I did?!" he says. "I got us out of there!"

"Good job," I say. "Just keep both eyes on the road."

"Don't worry, Wild. I'm really good with right turns and straightaways."

"I'm sure you are," I say. I reach for the seat belt, pulling it with my teeth and buckling it across my chest.

He glances over. "You trust me, right?"

"You drive a lot better than I do."

He smiles. "I'm glad there's at least one thing I do better than you."

Chance drives slowly down the road. A streetlight briefly illuminates the interior of the car, and I see a glint of something silver on the floor at my feet. I reach down and pull a laptop computer from under the seat.

"Look at this. They left their computer."

"We have to check it out," Chance says, reaching for it.

"One thing at a time," I say, pointing my muzzle back at the road.

"Right, right," Chance says, and he grips the wheel, concentrating hard.

"Drive for a little while, then we'll find a place to pull over and see what this is about."

"Will do," Chance says, and he takes a right onto Olympic Boulevard. Traffic is light, but there are enough cars around for me to feel like we're safe. At least for the moment.

"I'm glad you let me come with you," Chance says.

"I'm glad, too," I say, but my mind is racing to what comes next.

How can I keep us safe, figure out who is chasing us, and get Chance back home to his mother?

THE LAPTOP SCREEN GLOWS BLUE.

We're parked on the side of the road, examining the computer we found in the car. The initials CAT are emblazoned on the screen, superimposed on a shield insignia of some kind.

"What's CAT?" Chance asks, tracing the letters with his finger.

"CAT. It must stand for something. Can you get into the computer?"

He taps several buttons, but nothing changes. "The screen is locked," he says.

"Do we need a password?"

"Probably. But did you look at the keyboard?"

I look more closely and realize it's a bilingual keyboard— English and Cyrillic letters on each key giving a user the ability to type in Russian or English.

"That explains the accents," I say.

"This is way out of our league, Wild. Even you can't unlock a Russian computer."

He's right about that.

"Luckily we have a friend who knows a lot about computers," Chance says.

"I know what you're thinking," I say. "No way we're asking her."

"We have to. She's great at this stuff."

"Junebug is dangerous," I say.

"Her father is dangerous, not her. Anyway, she's changed. You haven't talked to her like I have."

I think about seeing the Finisher in the woods earlier and the very real prospect that Maelstrom is back in multiple forms.

I look at the laptop with its locked CAT screen and Russian keyboard, and I realize we're stuck.

Can I trust Junebug?

"Assuming we wanted to ask her about the laptop—how would we even find her?"

"Easy," Chance says with a smile.

We stand in the back of a school auditorium watching a chorus of girls in identical blue-and-gray uniforms sing. I stare at their faces until I find Junebug in the back row.

At least I think it's Junebug. Her hair is curlier, and she's dyed it a light brown. No more bangs or blue stripe down the side.

"Is that her?" I ask Chance.

"I told you she's way different now," he says. "It's kind of weird, right?"

"How did you know she'd be here?"

"I saw a post on her social media."

Someone in the crowd shushes us. A man leans toward Chance. "You can't have a dog in here," he says.

"Let's wait for her outside," I say, and I nudge Chance and trot toward the exit.

WE WATCH FROM BEHIND A DUMPSTER.

The concert ends, and the girls exit the back of the school, some in groups, some with family members who came to see them perform.

"There she is," Chance says, pointing.

Junebug is with two girls, all of them laughing as they walk through the parking lot.

"Stay here," I tell Chance. "Let me approach her first. Just in case things go bad."

"Fine," he grumbles, and slumps against the dumpster.

I step out from hiding, trotting across the lot until I get closer to the girls. They're completely absorbed in conversation, comparing notes about the concert.

I huff loud enough to get their attention.

"Whose dog is that?" one of the girls asks.

Junebug gasps when she sees me. "Is it you?" she asks. She looks into my eyes, then at my collar.

I bark once.

"WILD!"

"You know some random dog?" her friend asks.

"More than know her," Junebug says. "I'm crazy about her."

"You told me you hated dogs," her friend says.

"All but one," she says. "You guys go on without me. I'll see you in school tomorrow."

Junebug waves to her friends, and then her face lights up and she flings herself to the ground in front of me, laughing and burying herself in the fur on the side of my neck.

"I can't believe it's you!" she squeals.

Her energy is contagious, and I bark and jump, spinning around as she giggles and tries to grab me. She falls back, and I jump into her lap and allow her to cover me with strokes and kisses.

This isn't the Junebug I remember—the cautious, angry girl who guided Chance and me through trouble last year.

"Let me look at you," she says, and she takes my muzzle in her hands and stares at me adoringly. "Fancy new haircut. Me likey."

I lean down so she can open the hidden port in my collar.

She puts in an earbud and winces. "Wow, I forgot how much that hurts," she says.

"Can you hear me?" I ask.

She breaks into a grin. "Loud and clear," she says. "What's up, Wild? It's been a minute, right?"

"A minute and a half," I say.

She reaches down to close my collar port. "You know there's a bud missing in your collar," she says.

Chance steps out from hiding, and Junebug bites her lower lip, suppressing a smile.

"What's up, kid?" she asks, standing up to greet him.

"I'm not a kid," Chance says.

She touches Chance's long hair, brushing it out of his eyes. He blushes and backs up a step.

"Yeah, you look a little older since the last time I saw you. You even got some muscles."

"I've been playing soccer," he says.

"This is weird," Junebug says. "What's up with you guys? What are you doing at my choir recital?"

"We need your help," I say.

A black Mercedes pulls up behind us, capturing us in its headlights.

I growl and turn toward it.

"Easy," Junebug says. "This is my ride."

"It's not an Uber, is it?" Chance asks warily.

"Uber? No, it's owner," she says with a laugh. "My aunt owns the car and the driver is Gregory, our chauffeur. He takes me back and forth to school. It's my aunt's way of keeping an eye on me without having to do it herself."

"Your aunt must have a lot of money," Chance says.

"That's an understatement," Junebug says. "Do you guys need a ride?"

Chance looks at me for guidance.

Junebug licks her bottom lip, staring at us. "Something is up with you two. I can feel it."

A man in a dark suit steps out of the car. "Are you ready, Ms. Rupani?"

The driver has a Slavic accent that makes my hair stand on end. A rumble comes from deep in my throat.

Junebug reaches for me, patting my back. "Two friends are coming with us today, Gregory."

"Will do," the driver says with a nod, and he opens the back door for us.

"Hop in," Junebug says. "We can discuss on the way."

We climb into the back, and Gregory shuts the door behind us.

The seats are made of soft leather, and they smell of Junebug. I settle in, fighting the exhaustion that washes over me. I've been on the move since morning, and it's catching up to me.

It's not time to relax, girl.

I shake from head to tail, snapping myself back to attention.

"I have a million questions for you guys," Junebug says.

"We've got a few for you, too," Chance says.

The car glides through the night, flashes of streetlight illuminating the expensive interior. There's a privacy shield between the front and rear seats that separates us from the driver.

Junebug looks at the laptop clutched in Chance's hands. "What's with the computer?"

"That's one of the questions," Chance says.

"We shouldn't talk about this in front of the driver," I warn them.

"It's all right. He's a good guy," Junebug says.

"How long have you known him?"

She looks at me curiously. "He's been my aunt's driver for a decade, and he's been driving me for almost a year now." She puts a hand on my shoulder and lowers her voice. "Why don't you like him, Wild?"

"It's not him," Chance says. "It's the accent."

"He's from Ukraine originally," Junebug says. "What does his accent—"

"Let's talk about it when we get home," I say, unsure of what the driver can hear and wary of him seeing the kids talking to a dog in the back seat.

"Fine," Junebug says. "But I want to know what the mystery is."

"Don't we all," Chance says.

MY TOENAILS CLICK LOUDLY ON THE MARBLE FLOOR.

Junebug's house is so huge, it feels more like a hotel than a home. We walk past a grand piano in the living room, and she runs a finger across the polished wood.

"This place is like—I don't even have a word for it," Chance says. His voice echoes in the large space.

"My aunt's loaded," Junebug says with a sigh.

"You don't sound happy about it," I say.

"It's got pluses and minuses."

She heads up a carpeted staircase and Chance and I follow her into a bedroom. The scents are concentrated in here, a mix of Junebug's fruit shampoo and lavender sprayed on expensive sheets and blankets.

"Is this your room?" Chance asks.

Junebug nods. "My aunt's out of the house, so we can talk without worrying about anything."

Chance paces, uncomfortable.

"Why are you acting so weird?" Junebug asks. "You can sit on the bed if you want."

"No thanks," Chance says. "I don't like frilly stuff. I don't even sit on my mom's bed."

Junebug rolls her eyes. "Boys," she mutters.

Chance flops down in a big armchair and puts the computer on his lap.

Junebug looks back and forth between us. "What's the big secret, you guys? Fill me in."

"What do you know about a branch of Maelstrom called CAT?" I ask her.

"Cat? Like the animal?"

"CAT. It stands for something. I'm not sure what. Maybe they're Russian."

"Never heard of them. But listen, Maelstrom doesn't exist anymore," Junebug says.

Chance throws me a look.

"But your father—" I start to say.

"My father's gone. I haven't talked to him in almost a year."

"He's gone for good?"

"Don't know about that. I only know he called me once about a month after things went down at the beach last year. He wanted me to come back and live with him."

"What did you say?" Chance asks.

"I told him to shove it. He used me to hurt you. I don't care if he's my father. I'm never going back."

Her jaw is tight with determination. I can hear her heartbeat strong and steady. It seems like she's telling the truth.

"Where's your dad now?" Chance asks.

"My aunt said he moved to Boca Raton, so unless Maelstrom is based at a gated community in Florida, you guys have nothing to worry about."

Chance and I exchange glances. I think about the men chasing us with their knockout spray and tech devices.

If they weren't Maelstrom soldiers, who were they?

Junebug runs her fingers through my fur. "Why are we talking about Maelstrom, or Russians, or cats? What does that have to do with you?"

Chance comes over with the laptop and holds it out to her. "We need to break into this computer. It belongs to those CAT guys we were talking about," he says.

"You stole their computer?"

"No way. I don't steal computers. But I guess I stole their car and the computer was in it."

"Whoa, dude. What happened to you? You used to be scared of your own shadow."

Chance frowns. "Not true. Anyway, can you get us in or not?"

Junebug hesitates. "The thing is, you guys—" She stares at the floor.

"What's wrong?" I ask.

"I don't really do that anymore."

"You don't hack?"

"Not so much," she says. "My aunt made me promise I would give it up if I was going to live with her. I'm in the STEM program at my new school. I'm much more into app design now. I want to make money in a few years, become a start-up founder and all that. It's more interesting than the black hat stuff... and jail."

I look around the room, taking in the wall of books and the posters of female astronauts and scientists.

"Nobody even calls me by my hacker handle anymore. They just call me Jasmine."

"Do you want me to call you Jasmine?" Chance asks.

"No, I like when you call me Junebug. Both of you. It reminds me of the old days. But if you don't mind, I'd rather not hack if I can avoid it."

"We're in trouble," I say.

"Oh." Her face goes pale. "Is that why you came out of hiding, Wild?"

I nod.

"She showed up this afternoon," Chance says. "I was as surprised as you. That's when the trouble started."

"What kind of trouble?" she asks.

Chance gives in and sits next to us on the bed. "Someone is after Wild. And me, too, I think. We had to run away from my mom's apartment."

Junebug sucks in a breath and puts her elbows on her knees, thinking hard.

"Give me the stupid laptop," she says. She takes it to her desk and opens it, fingers poised over the keys.

"Are you sure about this?" Chance asks.

"What my aunt doesn't know won't hurt her. Besides, I'm not going to let anything happen to you." She studies the keyboard, running a finger across several keys. "I see what you mean about the Russian stuff. But let me give this a try." She

ALLEN ZADOFF

presses the space bar and the CAT logo appears on-screen. "That's the cat you've been talking about," she says. Junebug pushes a few buttons, then quickly pulls her fingers back from the keyboard. "Whoa. Not good." She picks up the laptop and studies it on all sides, then she puts it down again.

"What's the problem?" I ask.

"There's a port for a biometric sensor."

"Translation for smart people who don't care about tech?" Chance asks.

"Like a fingerprint reader that they can plug in to access the system. Without that, you need a password."

"So let's figure out the password," Chance says.

"It could be in Russian or English," she says.

"Could we try a few things?" I ask.

She shakes her head. "I'm sure this is an encrypted hard drive, Wild. Depending how tight they've made their security protocols, we probably get three failed password attempts before the laptop erases itself." She closes the lid. "I'm sorry. There's just no way. Not unless you want to lose all the data."

"There has to be a way," Chance says. "You would never have given up so easily a year ago."

"And you weren't so pushy a year ago," she says angrily.

"I was kidnapped earlier today and smuggled onto a plane," I say. "I don't know where they were taking me, but I don't want to find out."

Junebug sucks in a breath. "This is serious," she says.

"Very serious."

She sits quietly, pondering. "I have an idea, but you might not like it."

"I'm open to anything," I say.

"I'm not sure you're going to be open to this," she says, and she motions for us to follow.

We go down into the kitchen, where the driver is getting a snack.

"Gregory, can I talk to you for a second?" Junebug asks.

"Why are you talking to him?" I ask.

She shushes me and steps outside with Gregory. When she comes back, she's alone.

"Good news. Gregory knows some people who might be able to get us into the computer."

"Your driver knows computer people?" Chance asks.

"Obviously," she says. "But we can't go until tomorrow night."

"That's a long time from now," I say.

"You both look exhausted, and I need some food," Junebug says.

My mouth waters at the mention of food. "You might have a point," I say.

"But where will we sleep?" Chance asks.

"We've got six bedrooms in this house and only two of us live here. You've got plenty of choices."

Chance looks at me. "What do you think?"

"It's late and there's nothing much we can do anyway. We might as well get a good night's sleep and relax a little. Then we can figure this out together tomorrow night."

"It's a deal," Junebug says excitedly. "I'll go make us some sandwiches."

Chance's phone buzzes with an incoming message.

"Shoot, I have to tell my mom something, or she's going to freak out when I don't come home."

"Tell her someone pulled a fire alarm at the apartment and you had to take me back to my owners," I say.

"That will totally work," Junebug says.

"Do you ever stay at a friend's house?" I ask.

"Sometimes," Chance says.

"You still do sleepovers? How cute," Junebug says.

"They're not sleepovers. It's team bonding stuff."

"Do you guys wear matching soccer pajamas, too?"

"Super not funny right now."

I interrupt them with a bark. "Tell your mom that you're staying at your friend's house and you'll call her in the morning."

"Will do," Chance says. He sneers at Junebug, then starts to text, his thumbs moving at lightning speed.

"I'll grab some food, then maybe we can watch a movie or something," Junebug says. "Meet me downstairs in a few minutes."

WE DRIVE THROUGH THE DARK STREETS OF LOS ANGELES THE NEXT NIGHT.

We're in the Mercedes again with Gregory at the wheel, and Chance and Junebug are by my side in the back seat.

"How does Gregory know these people?" I ask Junebug.

"First, he speaks Russian and we need that. Second, he was a tech guy back in his country. He told me the story a while ago."

"What kind of a tech guy?" I say.

"A good one," Junebug says with a smirk. "Like me."

The partition window slides open, and Gregory talks to us over his shoulder. "Almost there," he says.

His accent makes me think about the men in the plane yesterday.

He glances at me in the rearview mirror. "The dog. She doesn't like me," he says.

"It takes her a while to warm up to people," Junebug says. "She'll get used to you."

"Maybe I'll give her a treat later, then she'll like me."

"Probably not," I say.

"I'm sure that'll help," Junebug says, holding up a finger to shush me.

"Okay, this is the place," Gregory says, and he pulls into a Dunkin' parking lot.

The three of us stare out the window.

"A doughnut shop?" Chance says.

"Don't judge a book by its cover," Gregory says with a smile, and he turns off the car.

THE DOUGHNUTS GLISTEN IN THE CASE IN FRONT OF US.

We're standing in an empty Dunkin' on Fountain Avenue near West Hollywood. I keep one eye on Gregory and one on the delicious-looking doughnuts, embarrassed by the loud rumbling in my stomach.

The clerk looks at us with a bored expression. "What can I get you?"

"Three glazed, two chocolate, and a half jelly," Gregory says.

"A *half*?" the clerk says.

"You heard me right."

"Welcome," the clerk says, and he nods toward the door behind him with an Employees Only sign above it.

"Follow me," Gregory says to us.

"What's going on?" Chance whispers.

Junebug shrugs. "This part's a mystery to me, too."

I look back to see the clerk reach under the counter and

press a button. The door buzzes, a lock clicks, and Gregory pushes it open.

I walk into a wall of delicious and unusual-smelling hot food, combined with alcohol and men who are drinking it. A bunch of guys sit at a long bar while another group plays cards at a big table in a corner of the room.

"*Pryvit*, my friends!" Gregory calls.

"*Pryvit!*" several men shout in response.

"Gregory, it's been too long," a man at the card table says. He's older with graying hair, and I can see he commands the respect of those around him. "The last time I saw you, you weren't even married. And now you have a family and a dog, too!"

Gregory laughs. "They're nice kids, but they're not mine, Ivan."

"What is this place?" Chance asks.

"It's like a community center, a home away from home for our people," Ivan says.

"Why is it hidden in a doughnut shop?" Junebug asks.

"Americans love doughnuts, so we give them what they love, and nobody asks questions. You understand?"

"I think so," Junebug says.

"Is Indy 500 in the back?" Gregory asks.

"He never goes home," Ivan says. "No matter how much I beg him to take a shower." He laughs and points to the doorway in the back. "Follow the smell. And don't be a stranger, Gregory."

We walk through the crowd, and the men greet us with

smiles. One of them reaches out with a tray of what look like dumplings. He eats one and offers another to me. It smells good, so I gobble it down, enjoying the hot potato filling inside.

"How is it?" Chance asks.

"Delicious!" I say.

"These are *vareniki*," Gregory says.

"What's that?" Junebug asks.

"Ukrainian dumplings," the man says, holding out the dish to the kids.

Chance takes a bite. "Amazing!" he says.

We thank the man and continue down a staircase and into a long hall with a door at the end.

"Let me do the talking," Gregory says. "He's the cousin of a friend of mine, but he's not so good with people."

"How is he with dogs?" I ask, and Chance shushes me.

"Here we go," Gregory says, and he takes a deep breath and opens the door.

The hum of electronics buzzes through the room. A skinny young man sits in a red seat that looks like it's been removed from a racing car. There are racing posters all over the walls—drivers posed in front of cars, their jackets emblazoned with the logos of many sponsors.

The young man types rapidly on a keyboard, looking across a bank of computer monitors that fill the desk in front of him.

"Indy, it's me," Gregory says. "Your cousin Alexi's friend."

The young man glances up and catches our reflection in

a monitor, but he doesn't look at us directly. Then he goes back to typing.

"Indy?" Gregory says.

No response.

Junebug gestures that she wants to give it a try, and Gregory motions for her to go ahead. She sidles up to the racing chair and whistles.

Indy keeps typing.

"Wow, you got all those 4K monitors daisy-chained together," Junebug says.

"No, 6K monitors. Not that I need the resolution, but you know—"

"Better to have and not need than need and not have."

Indy grins and taps a button. Every screen goes black at the same time, and he whirls around in his chair.

"What's your name?" he asks.

"They call me Junebug."

"You know your way around a processor, Junebug?"

"Sure do." She unzips Chance's backpack and takes out the CAT laptop. "But this one is out of my league. And Gregory told me you're the guy."

Indy looks at us directly for the first time. I imagine it must be strange to have kids and a dog walk into your hacker lair with no warning. Then again, we're in a secret Ukrainian social club in the back of a Dunkin'. Things are already pretty strange.

"Let me see the laptop," Indy says.

Junebug puts it in front of him, and he hesitates, fingers hovering above the keyboard.

"Russians," he says.

"Not the good kind," Gregory says.

Indy pulls a cable from behind the desk, plugs it in, and starts on the laptop. He's met with the same lock screen that's been stopping us.

"CAT. Never heard of it," Indy says.

"I didn't want to go any further than the screen," Junebug says. "I don't speak Russian, and if I can't find something with a familiar-looking name or folder structure... you know?"

"You did the right thing," Indy says. A few more taps and the screen fills with tiny lines of code.

"It's a custom OS. Loosely based on Linux," he says.

"What's he talking about?" Chance asks.

"It's a Russian-made machine," Junebug says. "It's got a different chip than our laptops."

Indy slaps his thigh and laughs. "I'm in! Now I know what CAT stands for," he says. "It's an acronym in English. CAT: Canine Action Team."

"I thought it was a Russian laptop," Chance says.

"Everything is in Russian except the organization's name. It's like a joke for them. Use English words to describe a Russian operation."

"Has anyone heard of the Canine Action Team?" Junebug asks.

Heads shake around the room.

Canine Action Team. I comb my memory, but there's nothing familiar about the name.

Indy scrolls through several screens, and his expression

turns serious. "These are bad people," he says. He taps a few keys and sucks in a breath. "Very bad."

"What's all this data?" Junebug asks. "They look like scientific papers."

I glance at the equations running down the screen.

"Genetic research," Indy says.

"Research on what?" Chance asks.

Indy points at me. "Dogs."

The servers along the wall come to life, clicking loudly, and Indy's monitor goes haywire with lines of code racing down the screen.

Indy screams and leaps out of his chair. He starts cursing in Ukrainian and yanking plugs from the wall. Gregory is talking to him rapid-fire, panic in both their voices.

"What's happening?" Junebug asks.

"They're here! They're in my system!" Indy yells.

He gives up on the plugs and dives for a red switch on the wall. He yanks it down and a bell rings through the bar, accompanied by the sound of shouts and running feet.

"Get out of here!" he screams.

"But we need your help," Junebug says.

He slams the laptop closed and pushes it into her arms. "Sorry, I can't help you."

The door bursts open, and two men in suits race in. Without a word, they guide us out of the room. I hear Gregory shouting behind us, but the men hustle us in the opposite direction, moving us down the hall. I could fight them, but I can see they're not trying to harm us, only get us out of there. They hurry us around the corner and through an exit door into the parking lot, then they disappear inside and slam the door behind them.

The Dunkin' sign blinks off and the store goes black.

"Whoa, what was that?" Junebug says.

"Something scared them," I say.

"What did he mean when he said they were in the room?" Chance asks.

Junebug holds the laptop in front of her like it's radioactive. "He plugged this into his system so he could install some tools, and I think they traced it back and broke through his firewall."

Gregory comes jogging around the corner. "I'm so sorry. I had no idea they would toss you out."

"What happened in there?" Junebug asks.

"These are not good people, the ones on the laptop. They are animal hackers, thrown out of Mother Russia. Exiled. Their own country does not want them."

"What's an animal hacker?" Chance asks.

"Genetic scientists." He points at me. "They hacked the dog DNA, you understand?"

"Why are they trying to capture Wild?" Junebug asks.

Gregory lowers his voice. "She is special, no?"

"Very special," Junebug says.

"Maybe they want to use her."

"For what?" Chance asks.

Gregory looks up. There's a Puppio billboard high on the wall of a nearby building.

THE DOGS OF THE FUTURE

"Everyone wants a special puppy now," Gregory says. "It's the puppy war."

I'm thinking about the Puppio signs, the Canine Action Team, the little device they used to identify my DNA. I feel like I'm on the verge of understanding what's happening, but the big picture is still beyond my grasp.

"I need to get you home," Gregory says to Junebug. "I'll pull up the car."

"Wait," she says, and she puts up a hand to stop him. "I'm staying with my friends."

"You can't do that," Gregory says to her.

"You told us the people in there are like family to you," Junebug says.

"It's true. But I work for *your* family."

"What are you doing?" I ask Junebug. "You have to go home."

Junebug shushes me, and Gregory looks down curiously, alerted by my whining. I trot in place, frustrated that I can't argue with Junebug right now.

"You put yourself on the line to help us," Junebug says, "and now your friends are in trouble."

He hesitates. "I can't—"

"If you want to help me, tell my aunt I'm staying at Cynthia's house tonight."

She takes his arm and walks him back toward the doughnut shop, talking to him all the way. After a heated exchange, he relents. They hug briefly, and he disappears around the back of the shop.

"Why did you send him away?" I ask Junebug.

"Because I'm staying with you," she says firmly.

"I've got one person's life in my paws," I say. "I don't want two."

"You owe me," she says.

"Owe you how?"

"I got you this far. You'd have no idea about CAT without me."

"She has a point," Chance says quietly.

"Admit it," Junebug says. "You need me."

"That's what I said," Chance mutters.

I bark in frustration and walk in a circle. There has to be a better way than taking them with me, but I can't think of one. Not out in the open in a Dunkin' parking lot.

"We can't have this conversation now. The CAT guys obviously know about this place, and we're standing in front of it."

"Good point," Chance says nervously.

I hear the whine of brakes behind us, and I turn to see an LA Metro bus pulling up at the bus stop across the street.

The three of us look at one another, and we start running for the bus at the same time.

Junebug hops on with Chance right behind her. Then Chance motions for me to jump up.

"Wait," the driver says. "You can't bring your dog on the bus."

"I'm taking her to the vet," Chance says.

"She doesn't look sick—"

"It's an emergency," Chance says, and he takes me by the collar and walks me onto the bus.

The driver mumbles and closes the door.

The three of us grab a seat at the very back of the bus, watching as the unlit Dunkin' sign recedes behind us.

"WHAT ARE WE GOING TO DO?" CHANCE ASKS.

He's staring out the window, and I can see the fear on his face in his reflection.

"I'm going to find out what these CAT people want," I say.

"How are you going to do that?" Junebug asks.

"They could be anywhere," Chance says, his voice growing tense. "They could be on this bus."

"Easy now," Junebug says. "I'm pretty sure these are normal folks."

I look around and see a few Angelenos minding their own business—an older woman with a paper bag of groceries on her lap, a man slumped against the window napping.

"Okay, okay," Chance says, and he takes a breath. "Back to my original question. How are we going to find CAT?"

I put a paw on Chance's backpack. "Think about it. We still have their laptop."

"And?" Chance asks.

"And they're going to want it back," I say.

Junebug smiles and claps her hands together.

"I don't get it," Chance says.

"We broke into their system," Junebug says, "so all we have to do is connect to a network somewhere."

"And they'll come to us," I say.

"We can set a trap for them," Chance says, catching on. "But won't that be dangerous?"

Chance and Junebug are both staring at me, waiting for an answer.

I have to think of a way to set a trap for CAT, but I don't want the kids anywhere near me when I do it.

"I'll figure this out," I say. "Nothing for either of you to worry about it."

"Right," Chance says. "I'll just relax and do some homework while we flee from Russian hackers."

"You have to admit it's kind of exciting," Junebug says.

"Exciting for you," Chance says. "You like this kind of stuff."

"I don't like it, I just—I guess I got used to it when I lived with my dad."

The bus empties out slowly as it moves along its route. I sit on the floor at Chance's feet, enjoying the vibration of the wheels going over pavement. I yawn, exhausted as the weight of the day hits me.

I look up at Chance and Junebug whispering together, piled into the seat above me. Chance reaches down and absentmindedly strokes my ears.

"It feels like old times," Junebug says with a smile. "We're in trouble, we're running—"

"And we're together," Chance says.

I sigh in pleasure, and Chance scratches me harder.

"It's kind of nice, right?" Junebug asks him.

Chance shrugs.

"Admit it," she says.

"I don't want to admit it."

I lean into the kids' legs, and Junebug scratches my back while Chance continues on my head.

"By the way," Chance says, "who's that girl you mentioned to Gregory?"

"Cynthia. She's just a friend from school. I hang at her house sometimes."

"Kind of like a sleepover?" Chance says with a smirk. "Because you're getting a little old for those."

Junebug laughs. "I deserved that."

The scratching is making me sleepy. I stand up and shake myself off, not wanting to let my guard down. Just because we're in motion doesn't mean we're safe. Not yet at least.

Junebug looks down at me. "You said you've only been with Chance for one night. Where were you before that?"

"Living with a family. Many families, actually. I moved every few months."

"Why didn't you stay in one place?"

"I was afraid Maelstrom would find me. I assumed they were hunting for me, and if I stayed put, I'd be easier to find."

"But you never saw Maelstrom?" she asks.

I think about the Finisher's eyes looking at me from the woods earlier today.

I consider telling the kids, but I don't want to panic them unnecessarily. They've been scared enough for one night.

"I never saw them," I say.

"But you still kept moving?" Chance asks.

"I tried to stay with a few families. Truth is, it was hard for me."

Chance looks confused. "Weren't the families nice?"

"They were okay. But it's hard to live with people who don't know who you really are."

"You didn't tell them you could talk?" Chance asks.

"I couldn't risk their safety or my own, so I just pretended I was a normal dog."

"Yeah," Junebug says wistfully. "I'm sick of pretending I'm normal, too."

"Seems like you have it good at your aunt's house," Chance says. "You have a driver and everything."

"My aunt's really nice," Junebug says, "but she's clueless. You know what she gave me for Christmas last year? A sweater. With butterflies on it."

"Is that bad?" Chance asks.

"I'm thirteen years old. I don't wear butterfly sweaters. Someone who knew me would know what I wanted."

"New iPhone?" I say.

"See what I'm talking about? Thank you, Wild."

She gives Chance a push on his shoulder. "What about

you? You're back with your mom, right? So at least your story has a happy ending."

"Kind of," Chance says. "I guess I thought it would be different."

"Different how?"

"My mom's back from treatment, but she's at recovery meetings all the time. I know it's a disease and everything, but all she does is go to meetings and talk to people on the phone."

"That sucks," Junebug says.

"Right? And when she's not doing recovery stuff, she's at work. It's like her life used to be about drugs and now it's about recovery. But you know what it's not about? Me. It's never about me."

Chance's face is red, and he clenches his fists in his lap.

Junebug puts a hand on his forearm, and Chance looks at her.

"You don't have to feel sorry for me," he says.

"I'm not. I'm just being a friend."

The bus pulls to the curb and the doors open to let a few passengers off. A mother with a baby girl strapped to her front gets on and sits a few seats away from us. The doors close and the bus continues down the street.

The baby coos and squirms against her mother's chest.

"She's a cutie," Junebug says.

"Thanks," the mom says. The baby grasps her finger and tries to put it in her mouth. "She's getting strong, too."

Chance jumps up. "Look!" he shouts, pointing out the window.

There's a park across the street lit up with floodlights, families with children eating tacos from a line of food trucks. A sign is hung between two trees in the front of the park.

Puppio Family Fest

"That's the company Gregory was telling us about earlier," Chance says. "He said there was a puppy war, remember?"

Chance reaches for the tape above the seat, signaling the driver to stop.

"What's going on back there?" the driver asks.

"We have to get out," Chance calls up to him.

"No can do," the driver says.

"My dog has to go to the bathroom, and she can't hold it."

The bus grinds to a stop, brakes squealing.

On the far side of the park I see a Puppio booth with a large digital display just like the one I saw at the dog costume contest. There are pictures of adorable puppies looking down from the display as if they're looking at the people walking by.

"Let's go find out about Puppio," Chance says.

Junebug looks at me, uncertain.

"You kids gotta get the dog off the bus," the driver shouts.

"Chance is right. Let's see what we can find out," I say.

"We're going," Chance shouts to the driver, and we pile off the bus and into the park.

WE WALK THROUGH THE CROWD TOWARD THE PUPPIO BOOTH.

An overly enthusiastic employee in a bright blue T-shirt greets us. "How are you folks tonight? Enjoying some human treats?"

Junebug fake laughs and rolls her eyes.

"What's a Puppio?" Chance asks.

The employee's mouth drops. "What? You haven't heard about us?"

"I've seen your ads everywhere, but I don't really know what it is."

"We've created the best puppies in the world."

"Second best," I say under my breath.

"Are you interested?" the man asks Chance and Junebug.

Chance looks at me. "I already have a dog," he says proudly, and I nuzzle his fingers with my snout.

"I'm sure your dog is very cool," the man says, "but these puppies are next level. You won't believe your eyes."

He pulls out an iPad and presses play on a video. We

watch an animation that shows a single cell growing into an embryo, and then the embryo is removed and scientists use DNA splicing to change it. After that, the embryo rapidly takes on the shape of a puppy in the womb. The animation cuts to live footage of a real Puppio dog like the ones on the digital billboards. Tiny bodies, big heads with giant eyes and smiles on their faces. They look less like puppies and more like dolls come to life. I shiver, my instinct warning me there's something wrong with these dogs.

But the humans around me have a different reaction. They crowd the table, making cooing sounds and fighting to get a closer look at the puppy video. Even Chance and Junebug seem delighted with the puppy on the screen.

"Ask him if these dogs really exist," I tell Chance.

"Can I get a puppy like this?" Chance asks.

"You mean a *Puppio*. We don't call them puppies."

"Right, a Puppio."

"Not yet," the man says. "But soon. There's going to be an announcement in a couple days."

Junebug steps forward, interrupting. "Have you ever heard of CAT?" she asks.

The man hesitates, looking at her strangely. "Of course. Everyone has."

She throws me a surprised look. "What can you tell me about them?" Junebug asks.

"Not much," he says. "I'm not really a cat person. I love dogs too much."

"He thinks you're talking about the animal," I say.

"Thanks anyway," Junebug says, and we start to walk away.

I look back and see Chance hasn't moved. He's flipping through a Puppio brochure, transfixed.

I bark to get his attention.

"Hey," Junebug shouts. "We have to get going."

He drops the pamphlet and jogs back to us. "Sorry, they're just so cute."

"They're made in a lab," I say.

"Weren't you made in a lab?" Chance asks.

"That's rude," Junebug says.

"No, he's right. I was made in a lab, at least from what I've been told. But it's not fun when you don't have a real home or parents."

"No parents sounds okay to me," Junebug says.

"Not to me," Chance says.

"Anyway, let's change the subject," Junebug says. "Wild, what do you think Gregory meant by *puppy war*?"

"I'm guessing the CAT people and Puppio are in competition with each other."

"And the CAT people want you so they can get a head start," Chance says.

"Maybe. I can't be sure what they want."

"I'm gonna take a walk and see if I can find out more about Puppio," Junebug says.

"Why don't you ask Wild if that's a good idea?" Chance says.

"What do you think, Wild? We're in public, and I can ask questions that you can't."

"Okay, but stay close," I say.

"You got it," she says, and she walks into the crowd.

"You're just going to let her go?" Chance asks.

"She needs a minute."

I'm not thrilled with the idea of her going off on her own, but I could tell the conversation was upsetting her.

"Can we get something to eat?" Chance asks. "Those Ukrainian dumplings were good, but I didn't get enough of them."

I nod toward a nearby Puppio food booth, and Chance grabs a free hot pretzel for himself and some beef jerky for me.

"This Puppio has some cash," Chance says. "They're feeding the whole neighborhood. Even the dogs."

He offers me the jerky. I chomp down on it, enjoying the meaty flavor as it softens between my teeth.

"Do you miss the family you were living with before me?" Chance asks.

"Not so much," I say.

"That's kind of sad."

"I was just a regular dog to them, and when people get used to their dog, they don't treat her like she's special anymore."

"They didn't know the real you. It's like the kids on my team. Half of them think I'm a loser, but they don't know I went through a battle with Maelstrom."

"Sometimes it's better to be underestimated," I say.

"What do you mean?"

"If people underestimate you, it's easy to surprise them."

"That's a good point," Chance says.

"I figured if I kept my real identity a secret, I'd stay out of trouble."

"But trouble found you anyway."

"I guess it did."

"So maybe all of that trying to fit in was a waste of time."

Junebug catches up to us at a jog. "All clear," she says. "Just a lot of people gossiping about Puppio and out for some free food. They said the first dogs were going to cost a hundred thousand each."

Chance whistles. "Who can afford a dog like that?"

"People like my aunt," Junebug says.

He breaks his pretzel and offers her half. "Are you hungry?"

"Thanks." She takes a bite out of the pretzel. "So what now?" Junebug asks me.

"I have to tell you guys something, but I don't want to scare you."

Chance groans. "There's nothing scarier than when someone says they don't want to scare you."

"I think I saw the Finisher earlier tonight."

"The tracker dog from the mountain?" Chance says quietly.

I nod. Chance bites at his lower lip, and Junebug's breathing speeds up.

"I thought you killed him," Junebug says.

"He went over the cliff, but I couldn't see what happened after that."

"How could he survive falling off a mountain?" Chance asks.

"He's not a normal dog. He's a Maelstrom dog."

Chance swallows hard, and sweat breaks out on his forehead.

"If the Finisher came back, why didn't he attack you?" Junebug asks.

"I'm not sure," I say. "It seemed like he was stalking me."

"I'm confused," Chance says. "Maelstrom is gone, but the Finisher is back? It doesn't make sense."

"Not to mention Puppio and CAT," Junebug says.

"What do they have to do with one another?" Chance asks.

"They all want Wild," Junebug says.

"Not Puppio," Chance says. "They don't want her."

"Maybe you're right," Junebug says.

We're interrupted by the sound of kids shouting up ahead. On the far side of the park, a night game of soccer is in full swing.

"That looks like fun," Chance says wistfully.

Junebug kicks at the ground, and an old tennis ball rolls across the grass. "Look at this," she says, her face lighting up. "We need to blow off some steam, you guys. Who can think when they're so worried?"

"We don't have time for games," I say.

She picks up the ball and tosses it a few feet in front of her, inviting me to get it. "Are you sure?" she says.

"That's not fair," I say. I look at the ball, instinct roaring for me to grab it and bring it back. "Okay. Maybe just one throw."

"Awesome!" Chance says.

I race forward and snap up the ball, carrying it back and dropping it at Junebug's feet.

"Let me try," Chance says, and he grabs the ball and flings it away.

I sprint after the ball, hot breath in my lungs and the smell of crushed grass beneath my paws. It feels like I could do this forever, racing away only to have Chance's laughter call me back over and over.

Is this what life's like for a normal dog?

A normal dog plays in the park with her person, gets snacks, takes naps. She goes for walks with her person, does her business, barks at strangers to protect her territory.

A normal dog does all these things, and then she goes home.

I think about being a dog like that, a dog who enjoys life, who has a person, who has a home.

Could I be that dog with Chance?

Junebug throws next, and I retrieve the tennis ball from the grass and carry it back to her between my teeth. Chance holds out his hands to receive it, but I stop short and drop the ball to the ground.

"I'm sorry I stayed away for so long," I say. "I thought it was the best thing to do."

Chance's expression softens, and he kneels down so he's eye level with me. "I forgive you," he says. "But I missed you a lot." He smiles and holds my head gently between his hands.

"I missed you, too," I say.

"You two are so sappy!" Junebug says with a laugh, and she grabs the ball from between us. "Go out for a long one." She points deep into the park.

"You think you can throw that far?" I ask with a grin.

"Watch me," she says. She picks up the ball, jaw set in determination, then rears back and whips it as hard as she can, grunting with effort. "Get it, Wild!"

I take off, following the arc of the ball through the air. I'm almost on it when the ball catches wind and lofts even farther, hitting a tree at the edge of the park and bouncing at a sharp angle that carries it over the park fence and out of sight.

I memorize the trajectory and I race after it, leaping the fence on the outskirts of the park and skittering between trees, determined to find it in the dense forest beyond the park.

I sniff and maneuver through the trees, tracking the mix of my scent and the kids' scent, both of them lingering on bark and branches wherever the ball made contact. The patch of forest ends, and I pop out onto a quiet road behind the park. I'm laser-focused on the ball, wanting more than anything to grab it and bring it back to Junebug and Chance.

I see a flash of green moving across the pavement, and I dive after it, realizing too late that it's rolling under the wheels of an SUV on the road.

I stop in the middle of the road, startled by the sight of the black SUV with the Uber sign in the window.

It's not just one SUV. There are half a dozen vehicles, a mix of sedans and SUVs, all of them black, their windows tinted so it's impossible to see inside.

I gasp and turn, forgetting the ball, the fur standing up all over my body as my mind struggles to process what I'm seeing.

The doors fly open, and men in green coveralls step out and cut off my escape.

I spin around, looking for a way out. I ran farther than I realized, and the thick trees behind me hide us from the people in the park.

"All these cars," a man says. "It's like the pickup line at the airport."

The voice sends a shiver from my nose to the tip of my tail.

It's the Uber driver who captured me the other day. He's back in his suit, standing and looking at me with a pleased expression on his face. He's holding a can of knockout spray.

"We meet again," he says. "Isn't that what the hero says in your Hollywood movies?"

I think it's the bad guy who usually says that, but I don't tell him that. I'm still not sure if he knows I can talk, and I don't want to give myself away.

Instead I growl a warning.

"Easy now," he says, and he looks over my shoulder.

The CAT men in coveralls shuffle nervously in a circle around me, but they don't move in. I quickly assess my escape options. There's space between the cars, and the men don't have weapons drawn—I could vault over them, dart through the line of fake Ubers, and be back in the park before they realize what's happened.

"You're planning your escape," the Uber driver says. "I know how fast you are and how cunning. I have no doubt you can get away." He slowly lifts his hand and puts the knockout spray into his pocket. "We haven't been properly introduced. My name is Viktor, and I think you'll want to stay and hear my proposal."

Why would I stay?

That's when I hear Chance's shout. "Get off me!"

I whip around and see Chance and Junebug coming out of the woods led by two CAT men in coveralls. The kids' shouts are drowned out by the crowd noise on the other side of the trees.

"You can't just grab kids off the street," Junebug says.

"I'm not a kid," Chance says.

"Just go with it, okay?" Junebug says angrily.

One of the CAT men pulls out a can of knockout spray, but Viktor holds up his hand, and the man does not spray them.

"Wild, what's going on?" Chance asks.

"*Wild*. Is that what you call her?" Viktor says.

Chance realizes his error and closes his lips tight.

"Wild. How interesting. I had to turn around an entire plane because of her," he says. "And I hate flying."

"What do you want from us?"

"Who's the girl?" Viktor asks.

"A friend from school," Chance says.

"Maybe we should let her go," one of the men says.

"Too late," Viktor says. "She's seen us. She'll talk to the police."

"She won't go to the police," Chance says. "She knows how to keep a secret."

"Do *you* know how to keep a secret?" Viktor asks.

Chance doesn't respond.

"Put the kids in the SUV," he says.

They walk past me, leaving a good amount of space. I could attack, but am I fast enough to take out all four men, then the dozen or so around us along with Viktor? Could I do it without anything happening to Junebug and Chance?

I decide my best bet is to go along, get us into a single car, and reassess my options. There are only so many men they can put into one car, even an SUV. The odds will be better.

I turn to follow them, and Viktor clears his throat. He opens the back of the SUV.

"You ride in here," he says.

The back of the SUV is a reinforced cage. I growl and bare my teeth.

"Save it," Viktor says. "We already have your friends."

I hop into the back seat and Viktor closes the door behind me.

Chance holds his hand up to the cage door, and I lick him through it, trying to comfort him.

"Who are these guys?" he whispers.

"This is the Canine Action Team."

"This is the Russian hacking group? Why are they driving Uber?"

Viktor gets into the front seat, his driver next to him. Two other men slide into the back, one on either side of Junebug and Chance.

"We'll take our laptop back, thank you very much," he says.

He reaches back and holds out his hand, waiting.

Junebug takes it out of Chance's backpack and hands it over. "How did you know we had it?"

"There's public Wi-Fi in the park," Viktor says. "You didn't shut down the laptop—"

"You read the MAC address and found us on Wi-Fi."

"Even better. The laptop is programmed to ping us when it's online and report its location."

"Darn it," Junebug says. "I should have thought of that."

Viktor laughs and motions to his driver, who pulls out.

"I'm sorry," Junebug whispers to us.

"It's not your fault," I say.

Chance looks back at me, his face etched with worry. Junebug grasps his hand. "We'll get out of this," she says. "We always do."

"Stop talking back there," Viktor says. "You'll have plenty to talk about on the flight."

"The flight?" Junebug says. "Where are we going?"

"You'll see when we get there," Viktor says, and then he turns his back to us.

I have to get us out of here. But how?

OUR SUV IS PART OF A CONVOY OF VEHICLES.

I glance behind and see the park fading from view. I track the SUVs behind us, trying to figure out the best way to escape.

"Keep these guys distracted while I figure something out," I tell the kids.

Chance gives me a wink and turns toward the front seat. "You can't just kidnap us in a truck," he shouts.

"A truck? This is an Uber XL Black. You ride with style when you ride with Viktor."

Junebug rolls her eyes. "You gotta be kidding me."

"I know who you are," Chance says. "You're the people from CAT."

"Canine Action Team," Viktor says, and then he says something in Russian and the guards in the SUV laugh.

"Why did you name your organization after the wrong animal?" Chance asks.

The laughter dies down in the car.

"Wrong how?"

"Canine is a dog," Junebug says. "But your initials add up to cat. You named your dog organization after a cat. Get it?"

Viktor clears his throat and looks down, seemingly embarrassed.

"I named it before I'd finished my ESL lessons in this country."

"You didn't realize C-A-T spelled *cat*."

"Maybe I didn't think it through completely."

Chance giggles.

"We all make mistakes," Viktor says defensively.

"You made a mistake today," Junebug says. "You don't realize who you have here."

"I know exactly who I have. And what I have."

"Ask him what he's planning," I say.

"What's the big plan?" Junebug asks.

Viktor points at me. "Is the dog telling you what to say?" he asks.

"Are you serious? Dogs can't talk."

"You're not fooling me. She barks, and then you ask me a question." He leans over the seat and reaches for Junebug's ear. "What do you have there?"

"Don't touch me!" Junebug says, and slaps his hand away.

The guard next to her pins her arms.

"Leave her alone!" Chance shouts, and he tries to take a swing at the guy hanging on to Junebug, but his arm is caught by his own guard.

"Now, let's see—" Junebug struggles, but Viktor easily

reaches over and takes out the earplug. I hear static as the connection with Junebug breaks off.

Viktor holds up the earbud and examines it in the light.

"Fascinating," he says.

He reaches toward his own ear.

"That's gross," Junebug says. "It's got my germs on it."

He wipes the bud off on his sleeve, then he puts it in his ear. There's a pause before he howls in pain, grabbing at his jaw.

Junebug smirks.

She and Chance high-five, much to the displeasure of the men sitting around them.

"I've read about this amazing dog," Viktor says, "but I didn't know you could communicate directly with her." He looks at me through the cage. "May I hear your voice, beauty?"

"Don't say anything, Wild," Chance says.

I watch Viktor, hatred in my eyes.

"Speak to me," Viktor says. "I'm not a bad man. I only want to hear your voice."

He nods to the guard next to Chance. The man puts a hand on Chance's shoulder, squeezing in a claw motion. Chance grits his teeth against the pain as the man's fingers turn white with effort.

"Don't talk to him!" Chance says.

"No reason for your little friend to hurt," Viktor says. "I only want to have a conversation with you, Wild."

I can't stand watching Chance suffer. I open my mouth to speak—

"Watch out!" Junebug screams.

A van plows into the front of the SUV, hitting it at an angle and sending us spinning across the highway and slamming into a guardrail.

I hear brakes screaming around us and the sound of multiple crashes. When I look out the window, it appears that every CAT vehicle has been in a crash at the same time.

The SUV vibrates with the sound of a drill on a lock, and the back door suddenly pops open.

People reach inside, pulling me out.

"Come with us!" the voices say.

I bark and try to stay in the car, looking to see if Chance and Junebug are safe. I catch sight of Junebug reaching into the front seat, yanking the earbud out of Viktor's ear and putting it back in her own.

"It's okay, we're bringing the children, too," the voice says urgently, and I hop out in time to see the kids being led to a waiting van.

I sprint after them, leaping into the van as the door slams shut behind us.

I look out the window at Viktor stumbling out of the car, a trickle of blood on his forehead where he injured himself during the crash.

"Come back, Wild!" he shouts, but the van is already in motion, and we're quickly out of range.

It's dark inside and I'm still confused from the crash, but I look around, noting the people who are already caring for the children. I growl a warning as a man reaches toward Chance.

"I'm an emergency medical technician," he says. "Please let me help."

I back up, and he pulls out a piece of sterile gauze and uses it to clean Chance's face with alcohol. The same process is going on for Junebug nearby.

Flashlights crisscross the space as they check the kids for injuries.

These people have patches on their shirts, each of them on the left side at chest level. A round patch with bright blue letters, worn almost like a badge.

"It's going to be fine," one of them says. "We'll take care of you."

The flashlight crosses one of their shirts, and at last I can read the letters written inside the patch.

Puppio

A middle-aged woman in the front seat looks back at us, and I see her face reflected in the light. Her features are familiar, the small nose and dark-cropped hair, the serious look in her eyes.

"Dr. Pao!" I say, my tail wagging.

"Hello, Wild."

She wears a flesh-colored earbud, her voice translating through my collar and into my head.

I dart forward and lick her face, amazed to see her again. She smiles and gives the fur on my neck a playful tug.

"You're alive," I say. "You escaped from Maelstrom."

"That makes two of us," she says. "I'm alive and well, and so are you."

Dr. Pao is the scientist who created the technology that was stolen by Maelstrom. They took something good and made something bad of it, pushing out Dr. Pao in the process.

I sit back on my haunches, relieved by the surprising turn of events.

Chance groans next to me, and his eyes open. He blinks hard, struggling to focus.

"You're okay," he says, relieved.

He sits up fast, looking for Junebug.

She's lying on the floor next to him, tended to by the EMT who holds an ice pack to the back of her neck. She looks over at the two of us staring at her.

"It was just a little car crash. Why are you guys so worried?" she says and gives us a thumbs-up.

She stares at the front seat, rubbing her eyes. "Is that Dr. Pao?"

The doctor smiles. "You're safe now. All of you."

THE VAN HEADS
SOUTH THROUGH
SANTA MONICA.

Chance and Junebug are sitting up and drinking juice now, both of them closely monitored by the medical technicians.

"This is so weird," Chance says. "First Wild, then Junebug, now Dr. Pao. It's like a high school reunion, only I haven't been to high school yet."

"How did you find us?" I ask Dr. Pao.

"I've been looking for you for months," she said. "You were in a park near a Puppio booth a couple of days ago, something about a dog costume contest?"

"You wore a costume?" Chance asks, surprised.

"I'll tell you about it another time," I say.

"We registered your collar when you passed by the booth," Dr. Pao says. "That flagged your location for me. I've been trying to catch up to you ever since."

"Lucky for us you did," Chance says.

"*Lucky.* That's a good word for it," Junebug says, her voice tense. She trades looks with Dr. Pao.

"What do you mean, Jasmine?"

"I prefer if you call me Junebug."

"But you're General Rupani's daughter."

"She hasn't seen her father in over a year," Chance says.

"What I meant," Junebug says, "is how did you appear out of nowhere with a half dozen cars and force the CAT people off the road?"

"Those people are trying to sabotage my company," she says. "We've been at war with them for months now."

Is this the war the Russians were talking about on the plane?

"You said *we.* Who do you mean?"

"Puppio," Dr. Pao says. "I'm the founder and I run the company."

"You're in charge of Puppio?" Chance says, astonished.

I sense the tension in Junebug's shoulders, but I'm not sure why she's so upset at seeing Dr. Pao. I whimper and lean into her, trying to calm her.

"I can't believe it's your company," I say.

"We grew so quickly, some days I have trouble believing it myself."

"What happened to Maddie?" Chance asks.

Maddie was Dr. Pao's beloved labradoodle companion, the leader of a group of specialized dogs who were protecting the doctor the last time we saw her.

"She fought bravely," Dr. Pao says. "But unfortunately, she was wounded and she didn't make it."

"I'm sorry to hear that," I say.

"I had so much fun with her," Chance says sadly.

"Thank you for remembering," Dr. Pao says. "It was one loss of many in the battle with Maelstrom."

The van gets quiet as we remember the day the Maelstrom soldiers broke into Dr. Pao's compound, and we had to run for our lives.

"Ah, well," Dr. Pao says with a sigh. "That's ancient history. Let's talk about now. I think you'll find it much more interesting." She points out the front windshield.

Beyond the trees, a shiny corporate campus stretches across several acres. Modern white buildings with mirrored windows are surrounded by manicured gardens. There's a huge parking lot filled with cars off to one side. We pull up to the front gate, where two men in blue T-shirts wave to us. A moment later the gate slowly winds open.

"Is this Puppio?" Chance asks.

"Exactly," Dr. Pao says. "This is our corporate campus. We'll drive through the front entrance so you get the full effect."

"Stop the van," Junebug says.

"But we're almost—" Dr. Pao says.

"Stop!" Junebug demands.

Dr. Pao signals the driver, and they bring the van to a halt.

Junebug grabs for the handle and yanks open the door. She jumps out of the van.

"What's going on?" Chance shouts after her.

He hops out, and I go after him.

Junebug runs a few yards and stops, hands on her hips, breathing hard.

"What happened?" I ask.

Junebug's eyes are flitting back and forth, and I see the sweat on her forehead. "We don't even know where we're going," she says.

"We're going to Puppio," Chance says.

"What is Puppio? You never even heard of it until like ten minutes ago."

"Their billboards are all over town. But I didn't know it was Dr. Pao's company."

"She shows up out of nowhere, and we trust her?" Junebug says.

Dr. Pao clears her throat behind us. "Is something wrong?" she asks.

"Yeah, Junebug's being weird," Chance says. "Maybe she hit her head or something."

"I'm not being weird," Junebug says. She grins, instantly covering the fear she was showing a second ago. "Sorry to jump out of the van like that, Dr. Pao, but I'm not coming with you."

"Why not?" Dr. Pao asks.

"I don't do military compounds," Junebug says.

"This is Puppio headquarters. It isn't a military compound."

"Whatever," Junebug says. "I see gates, cameras, and a guard booth."

"Security guards. We're a biotech company. Like I told you, CAT has been—"

"I still have bad dreams from the last facility where I lived," Junebug says.

Junebug grew up under the watchful eye of her father, homeschooled and working for Maelstrom on the weekends. Like me, she was traumatized by life on a military base.

Dr. Pao shrugs. "What a pity. I was excited to show everyone the research labs—you especially, Junebug. We have our own quantum processor. There are only a few in the world."

"It's tempting," Junebug says, "but I'm going to take a hard pass."

Dr. Pao shakes her head frustrated. "Talk to her," she whispers to me, and she makes her way back to the van.

I wait until the door is closed, then I approach Junebug. "You think it's a trap?" I ask her.

"I don't know what it is," she says. "But with guards and gates and all this talk of war—I don't want to find out."

"Dr. Pao saved us from CAT," Chance says. "She fought Maelstrom with us. Did you forget?"

"I remember everything," Junebug says. "But I'm still not going in."

"I get it," I say. "We can't force you. Maybe you'll let them drive you home. It's late and it's dark out."

"I'm good," she says. "I'll call Gregory once I get down the road a little. Don't worry about me, Wild. I can take care of myself."

I know Junebug is strong, but she's still a thirteen-year-old girl.

I open my mouth to talk to her, but her face is determined, and I know how stubborn she can be.

"Call Chance's cell if you need us," I say.

"Got it," she says.

"You're just gonna let her go?" Chance asks.

Junebug looks my way.

"I'll see you when I see you, kid."

"Don't call me kid." Junebug reaches for her earbud.

"You want to hang on to it?" I ask her.

"You might need it. And I can always put it in again the next time we meet." She opens my collar port and replaces the bud. "It was really nice to see you again, Wild." She strokes the side of my face one final time, then she heads down the dark road.

"I can't believe she's leaving us," Chance says.

"She's been through a lot."

Chance frowns. "We've all been through a lot. You still don't leave your friends."

"Try to take it easy on her," I tell Chance.

The van engine starts up behind us.

"Let's get inside," Dr. Pao shouts to us through the window.

I nod to let her know we're coming. But neither Chance nor I move.

"What do you think?" Chance whispers.

I don't do military compounds, Junebug said.

I scan the length of the Puppio facility—high fence, a guard house, and crash barriers set up to prevent traffic from bypassing the guards. There's no doubt it's a secure facility, but it looks like a corporate campus, not a military base.

Dr. Pao is sitting in the van waiting for us. She seems uptight but friendly, just like the Dr. Pao I remember.

"I think we should see what this place is all about," I tell Chance.

"Right, what's the worst that could happen?"

And with that, we climb into the van for the short drive into Puppio.

WE WALK DOWN A LONG, STERILE HALLWAY BORDERED BY OFFICES AND LAB SPACES.

The tile beneath my feet is free of scuff marks and the walls smell like fresh paint. Whatever is going on here, it hasn't been going on long. Scientists in white coats look up as I pass by, staring at me and whispering.

"Do they know me?" I ask.

"They've heard stories about you," Dr. Pao says. "You're like a hero to them."

"Why is she a hero?" Chance asks, his head on swivel.

"Wild was the precursor to a lot of our work here."

"Precursor?"

"Sort of like the one who started it all," Dr. Pao says.

"I was a Maelstrom dog. What does that have to do with anything happening here?"

"Maelstrom stole their technology from me, remember? They used it to do bad things, but the basic concept was good."

"What concept?" Chance asks.

"To create a dog better than any that came before. A dog like Wild."

"I'm not better," I say. "I'm just me."

"Really? How many people are having a conversation with their dog right now?" Dr. Pao asks.

"And their dog is answering!" Chance says with a laugh.

I snort, uncomfortable with the conversation.

I look at the maze of hallways, the dozens of offices, the doors sealed with secure entry pads. I glance through windows and I see that despite the late hour, most of the offices are filled with Puppio employees hard at work.

"Do these people work all night?" I ask.

"Not usually," Dr. Pao says. "But we're on a tight deadline. Right now everyone is giving it one hundred percent."

I wonder what that deadline is, but it's one of about a thousand questions racing through my mind.

"We're already three times the size that Maelstrom ever was," Dr. Pao. "Three times as big and growing."

"Growing into what?"

"A cutting-edge tech company."

"I thought Puppios were a new dog breed," Chance says.

"They're more than a breed. Puppio is a movement, a revolution in how we think about our pets. You'll understand soon enough," she says.

She gestures to a vast laboratory area in front of us, where scientists and technicians hurry back and forth.

"This was my dream, Wild. It was stolen from me, and now I have it back."

Her face glows with delight. I can see how happy she is, and I want to be happy for her, but the place has me unsettled. I keep thinking about what Junebug said outside.

I don't do military compounds.

Dr. Pao stops at a door with a security pad at human-face height. She looks into the pad, a laser scans her retina, and the lock clicks open.

"I feel like I'm in a sci-fi film," Chance says.

"We have a sterile environment inside this area," she says. "No air transfer between sections. We need to be careful with our experiments."

Chance hesitates. "I don't like experiments."

"Do you like science class?" Dr. Pao asks.

"It's okay."

"Experiments are just science in action, a way of testing our ideas in the real world. I think you're going to be impressed."

"Junebug would be impressed. I'm just kind of along for the ride."

The doctor chuckles. "I get it. You know, Junebug and I are so much alike. We're both stubborn. She'll come around,

I hope. Now we come to the real reason I brought you here," Dr. Pao says.

"Real reason?" I ask.

Dr. Pao stops in front of an inner door framed by two security officers. "This is going to surprise you, Wild." She gestures and the guards step out of the way to let us through.

A MIST IS RELEASED IN THE PASSAGEWAY AROUND US.

I grunt, startled as the white cloud jets out from the walls and ceiling, surrounding the three of us in a fog.

"It's a disinfectant," Dr. Pao says. "So we don't introduce germs into this area."

The mist stops and a blast of cool air washes across us, clearing the passageway. The doors slide open, and we step into a large room that looks like a training facility at a gym.

I hear the sound of dogs yelping. There are two puppies playing on a large mat across the room, barking and pouncing through an impromptu game of king of the hill.

"Are those Puppio puppies?" Chance asks excitedly.

I can already see that they're not. They don't have the cartoonish features or big heads we've seen in the ad.

"Puppios? No, not exactly," Dr. Pao says.

They look like normal, mixed-breed puppies, possibly even siblings. One is brown with a white patch on his face, and the other is white with a brown patch. The puppies are several months old, in that awkward age between childhood and adolescence where a puppy starts to look like a young dog.

The brown puppy jumps nearly three feet in the air before landing in a tight crouch. The white puppy barks and darts away so quickly, she's nearly a blur. It's an incredibly athletic feat for such young dogs.

"They're strong," Chance says. "Kind of like you, Wild."

Dr. Pao calls to the puppies. "Scarlett! Sebastian! I want you to meet someone."

The puppies are so enthralled by their game, they don't immediately react to the doctor's call. First one looks over, then the other, and they sprint toward us, yelping excitedly. The brown pup trips over his feet and sprawls, falling over himself. The white pup stops, picking the brown one up by the scruff of the neck and pulling him to standing, before urging him to run with her.

They come to a stop a few feet away from us. Chance looks at them, delighted. "Can I play with them?"

"Let me introduce you first," Dr. Pao says.

She points to the white puppy. "This is Scarlett. And the brown pup next to her is Sebastian."

I sniff the air and I'm struck by a scent both familiar and strange. At first I think it's my own scent and that perhaps the disinfectant spray disturbed my sense of smell. But when I sniff again, I realize the odor isn't coming from me.

It's coming from the puppies.

I edge forward, not quite believing my own nose. I reach toward the white puppy, Scarlett, and she sneezes and backs up. Before she does, I get a good whiff of her.

"Does she smell familiar?" Dr. Pao asks.

"She smells like me," I say, confused. "They both do."

"How did your scent get on these puppies?" Chance asks.

"It didn't get on them," Dr. Pao says. "It's their natural scent."

I stare at the puppies—thinking about their brown-and-white coloration, the shape of their faces, and the strength in their young bodies.

"Is this the one you told us about?" Sebastian says.

I yelp in surprise. "They can speak?"

Dr. Pao grins. "They can do a lot of things," she says. She beckons them forward. "Scarlett and Sebastian, I'd like you to meet my old friend Wild."

"So this is Wild," Sebastian says, awe in his voice.

"Momma!" Scarlett shouts joyfully.

The room starts to spin before my eyes, and my heart races.

Away.

That's all I can think.

Get away.

I pivot and take off, gaining speed as I accelerate away from these puppies, their scent, everything about them.

"Wait!" Chance shouts.

But I can't wait. I'm panicking, my heart thundering in my chest, breath coming in short gasps. I smash into an emergency exit door and an alarm goes off, ringing through the facility.

I ignore it and run.

I RACE THROUGH
THE HALLWAY.

I run without knowing where I'm going, moving through the maze of a building I've never been in before. People pop their heads out of offices and look at me going by, but nobody moves to stop me. I get to the end of the hall and crash through another door.

I'm running blind, trying to get away from the scent of the puppies and what the smell might mean. The alarm cuts out and the hall goes silent, the only sounds my paws slapping on the tile and my breath roaring in my ears.

I burst into a fancy lobby area, large plate glass windows looking out to a visitor's parking lot beyond. I see the giant letters of the Puppio sign high up on the glass. We came into this building through a side door, but now that I'm up front, I see that Dr. Pao was telling the truth. This is a legitimate company, open to the public, designed to show off the Puppio brand.

It's not at all like the secret Maelstrom base hidden

underground in the mountains near Malibu where I fought General Rupani last year.

"I've only seen photos of you," a man says.

I spin around to find a young guy in a tight blue suit and expensive glasses looking at me from behind a reception desk.

"You're Wild, right?" he asks. "You're famous around here. You're the one who started it all."

He's talking directly to me, which means he knows I can understand him.

The puppies know me, the employees know me—

I turn away, looking out the large windows to the parking lot.

"I know it's a lot to take in all at once," Dr. Pao says. "The door is unlocked if you want to get some air."

She comes into the reception area with Chance by her side. She stays back, giving me plenty of space.

"Are you okay, Wild?" Chance asks, worried.

Pull it together, girl. You're scaring Chance.

I try to slow my breathing, but I can't.

A large video monitor on the wall shows a Puppio promotional video. The now-familiar Puppio cuties play together, bounding through an impossibly green field.

"Where did the two puppies inside come from?" I ask.

Dr. Pao turns to the desk. "Why don't you take a break, Peter?"

"But I'm working on a PowerPoint deck for our new business presentation."

"Now," Dr. Pao says sternly.

Peter leaves. I hear Dr. Pao breathing softly behind me, not moving closer but not going away. I stand at the door, looking out at the moon visible through the clouds.

"It was before your last mission," Dr. Pao says. "Maelstrom extracted your eggs and froze them in the lab."

"They stole her DNA?" Chance says.

"She was a Maelstrom soldier. They made her, so they felt it was in their right to take something from her."

"So those dogs in there—" I say.

"They're your puppies."

I sit back hard, my head spinning. When I ran away from my final mission for Maelstrom, I was zapped and left for dead. I lost my memory and my identity, and it's taken me a long time to get some of those memories back.

But I don't remember anything about these puppies.

"Did I know about them?" I ask. "Before I lost my memory?"

Dr. Pao shakes her head. "No. I found the records after they deserted their base in Malibu. It said that the last family you were with—the Horvaths—took you to a vet who told them you needed a minor surgery. They brought you in for the procedure, not knowing the vet was working for Maelstrom."

"That was the night I went rogue."

The night I attacked my handler. The night my war with Maelstrom began.

"The vet took your eggs during that surgery. There was some thought at Maelstrom that perhaps you suspected— even unconsciously. Maybe that's why you refused to hurt the children that night and carry out your mission."

"Maternal instincts?"

"Perhaps," Dr. Pao says.

"You said they took the eggs. But where did the puppies come from?"

"When Maelstrom disappeared, I found the records at their base along with your biological samples, and I used it to start Puppio."

"You grew the puppies?" Chance asks, wide-eyed.

"Yes," Dr. Pao says.

I turn to confront her, teeth bared.

She holds up her hands defensively. "I'm sorry, Wild. It was the only way. Otherwise I would have had to start over from scratch."

"You picked up where Maelstrom left off," I say.

"But with an entirely different mission," Dr. Pao says.

"What is your mission?" I ask.

She looks from me to Chance. "This is a longer conversation."

"Then let's make it a short conversation," I say.

"I promise I'll tell you everything you want to know," she says. "But right now those puppies need you. They don't know anything about Maelstrom, about the past, about the battles between you and General Rupani. They only know they're alive, they're special, and they need a mother."

I see Chance looking at me concerned. I want to push through the door and take him away from this place. But another part of me wants to go back into the training facility and get to know my puppies.

"What should I do?" I ask Chance.

"If you're really their mom, you should go and meet them," he says.

"I'm afraid, Chance."

He looks at me kindly. "Don't be afraid. I'll come with you."

I think about the brown-and-white puppies inside the facility. They smelled like me. They smelled like home.

"What are their names again?" I ask Dr. Pao.

She smiles and motions for me to follow her.

THE PUPPIES SNAP TO ATTENTION WHEN WE COME INTO THE ROOM.

They face the doctor with heads held high.
They sneak glances at Chance and me, but they're well-disciplined enough not to move without permission.

"Good evening, my young friends," Dr. Pao says.

"Hello, Doctor!" the puppies call in unison.

She beckons me toward the young dogs. I edge forward, sniffing.

"You came back!" Scarlett says, and she races forward, flinging her little head under my chin and snuggling up against me.

I have the same strange feeling I had earlier. I'm smelling another dog, yet I'm also smelling myself.

"You can't have her all to yourself," Sebastian says, and he scampers over, crouching in front of me, inviting me to play.

"How did you learn to talk?" I ask him.

"All dogs talk, don't they?"

I glance at Dr. Pao.

"They're still learning," she whispers.

Sebastian grabs Scarlett by the tail and pulls her away from me. "My turn," he barks at her.

She comes forward again, and her tail snaps Sebastian across the bridge of his nose. "Oops. Didn't see you there," she says.

The puppies sound like human children, but their grammar is already more sophisticated than children's, and far more advanced than even the smartest average dog.

"Who's that?" Scarlett asks, pointing at Chance with a tiny paw.

"That's my best friend," I say, and Chance blushes.

"What is this room we're in?" Chance asks.

"It's like their school," Dr. Pao says. "What are you learning today, Sebastian?"

"Today we learned how to call nine-one-one."

"How do you dial a cell phone with paws?" Chance asks.

"Not on a phone. On our collars!" Sebastian says with a laugh.

"Their collars will be tapped into emergency services."

"In case our person falls or hurts herself and she needs help," Scarlett says.

"Your person?" I ask.

"Everyone needs a person," she says, like it's the most obvious thing in the world.

I turn to Dr. Pao. "You're training them to be service dogs?"

"In a sense. We're training them so they can train others."

"Other what?" Chance asks.

"Sebastian and Scarlett will train the Puppio dogs," Dr. Pao says.

"Dogs training dogs?" I say.

"Amazing, isn't it? And they're smart enough to do it," Dr. Pao says.

"Sebastian's not so smart," Scarlett says, and Sebastian growls low, warning her.

"Be nice," Dr. Pao says. "You're brother and sister and you have to learn to get along."

Scarlett grumbles but backs away, sitting down next to her brother in a submissive posture, tongue out and eyes down.

"Say goodbye to Wild now," the doctor says.

The puppies surround me, yipping happily and leaping on top of me, wanting to play. I push them away and step back.

"What's wrong?" Scarlett asks.

"Don't you like us?" Sebastian asks.

"Of course I like you," I say, even though I'm not sure how I feel yet.

"Then let's play!" Scarlett says.

The puppies race around and nip at me. At first I feel like I'm being attacked, and then I realize their nips are harmless, their challenges a way of drawing me into play.

"You smell great!" Scarlett says.

"She smells like us," Sebastian says.

They tackle me, and we go down in a tumble of fur and happy puppy sounds. I give way to the sensation, letting the puppies cover me with licks and snuggles. As I let my guard down, I begin to experience a strange feeling, something I've never felt for another dog.

The feeling is so unexpected, I'm not sure what to call it.

"They love you already," Dr. Pao says.

Love.

That's the word I was looking for.

The doctor whistles, and the dogs disengage from me, coming to attention in front of Dr. Pao. She kneels and gives them warm pats on the head.

"Time for dinner," she says. "You can see Wild tomorrow."

They bark and race for the door.

"See you later, Wild!" Sebastian shouts.

A tangle of fur shoots through a low opening in the door, and the room goes quiet.

Dr. Pao sighs. "They have a lot of energy. It's hard to keep up with them sometimes."

Chance puts his hands on his forehead. "I can't believe they can speak. Or that they're Wild's kids. Or any of this."

"I'm having trouble believing myself." I look around the training facility and smell the lingering scent of the puppies. "This is why you brought us here?" I ask Dr. Pao.

"I brought you here to get you away from CAT. But in a

larger sense, you're right. This is why I've been looking for you for so long. It's why I wanted you back."

"So I could meet my puppies."

"More than meet them. They need you. You can teach them things I never can. How to use their senses. How to defend themselves. How to be dogs in a world that belongs to humans."

"Slow down," I say. I feel a nervous twitch in my cheek as I imagine working with the puppies.

"They'll learn about humans from a dog's perspective," Dr. Pao says. "You know more about that than anyone."

"It's true," Chance says. "You're practically human."

"They need you, and I need you, too," Dr. Pao says.

"Why do *you* need her?" Chance asks.

"She has all the science of Maelstrom within her," Dr. Pao says, and she kneels in front of me. "We can unlock that science together, Wild. We'll use it to make more dogs like you."

"The world doesn't need more soldiers," I say.

"Not soldiers. Intelligent, caring dogs who can help people. Dogs who know the difference between right and wrong."

"That sounds like you," Chance says.

I lock eyes with Chance, and I see the sadness on his face. I shake my head. "I can't stay at Puppio," I tell Dr. Pao. "I have responsibilities."

"I know you and Chance have a special bond," Dr. Pao says.

"More than special. He's my best friend."

Chance smiles thinly and scratches behind my ears.

"I understand," she says. "That's why I have a little surprise for Chance."

"I'm not sure I can handle any more surprises today," Chance says.

"I think you're going to like this one," Dr. Pao says.

THE DOORS OPEN.

The Puppio employee from the lobby enters with a large gift box with a blue ribbon on top. He carries it into the room and puts it on the ground at Chance's feet.

"I'm Peter," he says. "If you need anything while you're here, just let me know."

Dr. Pao nods her thanks. Peter stands to the side, watching while Chance looks at the box on the ground in front of him.

"Is this for me?" Chance asks Dr. Pao.

She smiles.

"What is it?"

She shrugs like she has no idea and gestures for him to open it.

"Is it okay?" he asks me.

"I guess so," I say.

Chance reaches for the ribbon on top of the box—

And the box moves.

Chance shouts and jumps back. I growl and rush forward. Dr. Pao puts out an arm to stop me.

"Nothing to be afraid of," she says. "Let him have the experience."

I look at her curiously, but she stays silent.

Chance tentatively reaches for the box again. He undoes the ribbon on top, and the front of the box immediately slides open.

A head pops out, startling us and causing Chance to shout and jump back.

I watch as a Puppio puppy sniffs its way out of the box and lets out a high-pitched yap. It looks just like the puppies on the billboards and the video displays.

"She's a beauty," Dr. Pao says. "And you're the first to meet her."

Chance screams in delight as the puppy shimmies out of the box, wagging its hindquarters, struggling to find its footing on the floor of the training facility.

"I'm the first?" Chance says. "Amazing!"

The puppy has white hair, massive bright blue eyes, and paws slightly too big for her frame. She sniffs the ground at Chance's feet, then sneezes and scares herself, backing away from the sound of her own sneeze. She gets tangled in her legs and falls onto her back, kicking the air momentarily before spinning around and coming back to standing.

Chance howls and Dr. Pao bursts into laughter. Even Peter can't help but giggle.

All puppies are cute, but this puppy is extraordinary, by far the cutest puppy I've ever seen.

Chance reaches down to pick up the puppy, but Dr. Pao cautions him.

"Don't grab her. Let her have a minute to smell you and get acclimated. This is the bonding process. It's shorter with our puppies, but it still requires a little patience."

Chance sits on the ground with legs out, waiting as the puppy sniffs her way over to him.

"Hello, girl," he says, and the breath catches in my throat. He's talking to the puppy the way he usually talks to me.

The puppy edges toward him, sniffing at his jeans. Then she yelps and nips at Chance's pant leg, wanting more attention.

"Now?" Chance asks.

"Perfect," Dr. Pao says. "Extend your hand, palm open."

Chance reaches out, letting the Puppio smell his open hand. The dog leaps into Chance's lap, cuddling against him.

Chance falls onto his back laughing, and the puppy jumps onto his chest, rolling over and squirming, spreading her scent on Chance's shirt, invisibly marking Chance as her owner.

"There you have it," Dr. Pao says. "They've bonded. It's as easy as pairing your iPhone."

"She smells GREAT!" Chance shouts.

I sniff the air and catch the scent of something familiar. More like a bakery than a puppy.

"She smells like an apple pie!" I say. "How is that possible?"

Chance buries his nose in the puppy's fur, breathing deeply.

"It's an unusual genetic enhancement," Dr. Pao says.

"The puppies smell like people's favorite foods. Each one a little different, based on the tastes of the person they've been selected for. Cupcakes, brownies, fruit pies, French toast. We're working on a line that smells like fresh baked bread. Things that are delicious to the human nose."

"How did you know what Chance would like?"

"I had a sample of his DNA."

"How did you get his DNA?"

"Last year when you were at my house," she says. "He touched a lot of things. We can determine preferences from the tiniest sample of skin or saliva."

"You saved his DNA?"

"I save everyone's DNA. I'm a genetic scientist, and I hoped to do a project like this one day, and I wanted to do it first for the people I care about."

"Dogs matched to owners by their DNA? That's so artificial," I say.

"It's the next big thing," Dr. Pao says. "It's like a search engine that knows what you want before you ask for it, or an online clothing store that predicts your taste based on previous purchases. We know what you're going to like because we know you from the inside out. Anyway, it seems to be working for Chance," Dr. Pao says.

She's right. Chance is completely obsessed with the puppy. He's on all fours playing with her as if he's another dog.

"We think people will prefer this smell to normal dog smell. Once they get used to the Puppios, the smell of natural dogs will fall out of favor."

I look at Chance rolling around on the floor with the puppy, and I feel a surge of jealousy.

"That's enough for now," I say to Chance. "Give the puppy back."

"But I'm having so much fun," Chance says. "Don't you want to meet her, Wild?"

"Fine," I say.

I trot forward and the scent intensifies. The puppy whimpers as I come close, crouching down. It leaps at me and I growl, sending it scurrying backward.

As it turns, I notice something on the back of its neck. Its fur is mismatched in one spot, almost like a scar that has been sewn together after surgery.

I have a similar scar.

I flash back to a time last year when we were being chased by Maelstrom. Everywhere we went, Maelstrom followed as if they were able to track me. Eventually, we discovered a microchip that had been implanted in my body.

A chip with the corporate logo for BreedX, the technology originally created by Dr. Pao and stolen by Maelstrom.

I stare at the Puppio dog and a chill goes through me as I think about that scar and the chip beneath it. A growl rumbles from deep in my chest, vibrating the air around me.

The puppy cowers behind Chance's leg, afraid to make eye contact with me.

"You're scaring her," Chance says, upset. "Stop it!"

I cut off the growl and make my voice steady. "We should let the puppy go back home now," I say.

"You don't understand," Dr. Pao says. "I'm *giving* the puppy to Chance. It's a gift."

"Forever?" Chance asks.

"Of course," Dr. Pao says.

Chance claps his hands together, delighted. All kids love puppies, but I don't like what I'm seeing across from me. Chance has only known this puppy for five minutes, and he's completely bonded with it. He was unsure a little while ago, but now he looks completely relaxed and happy.

"You're one of the first kids to see a Puppio dog in real life," Dr. Pao says. "And I think you should be our first owner, too. You deserve it after what you went through with Maelstrom."

I clear my throat, interrupting. "That's very nice," I say, "but he's not allowed to have dogs in his apartment complex."

"We've taken care of that," Dr. Pao says. "Landlords receive a generous payment to convert their buildings to Puppio-friendly residences. It's part of our business plan. We just got off the phone with Chance's landlord, and he was very happy to accept the money."

"We need to talk about this," I tell Dr. Pao.

"Can I keep her?" Chance asks. "Please, Wild. Please, please?"

I see his face glowing with joy, and it makes me feel uncomfortable. "You can keep her for now," I say, unsure about this new dog.

"Does she have a name?" Chance asks Dr. Pao.

"I think you should give her one," she says.

Chance studies the dog. "I'm going to call her Big Eyes. Maybe that's dumb because it's so obvious—"

Super obvious, I think, but I don't say anything.

"Big Eyes is a great name," Dr. Pao says.

I grumble as Chance stands and holds out his hands, and Big Eyes leaps into his arms.

"I bet you're hungry," Chance says.

Peter steps forward. "I'll show you where the cafeteria is."

"Be gentle with her," Dr. Pao says. "She's still learning."

"I promise," Chance says. "Come on, Big Eyes!"

He cradles the Puppio and follows Peter out the door, leaving without even bothering to say goodbye to me.

As soon as he's gone, I whip around and confront Dr. Pao. "You can't just give him a dog. You need to get permission from his mother." I can hear the anger in my voice, even as I try to hide it.

"People can't resist the Puppios. I don't think his mother is going to be a problem. And you saw how excited he was."

I snort and walk in a circle, burning off excess energy.

"You seem upset," Dr. Pao says.

"I'm not upset. I'm surprised," I say.

"With Scarlett and Sebastian in the picture, you have something to care for now. Chance needed something, too."

"We've always taken care of each other," I say.

"I'm not trying to take that away from you. But what is Chance going to do now that you're a mother and have responsibilities?"

"I haven't decided—"

"Decided what?"

Whether I'm going to stay at Puppio, I think.

But what else can I do? Am I really going to abandon my puppies?

I try to think clearly about the situation, my puppies, the new Puppio dog, but I'm overcome with exhaustion.

"I need to get some rest," I say.

"I think that's a good idea," Dr. Pao says. "We've got sleeping quarters for you and Chance for the night, and we can talk this through in the morning."

"In the morning," I mutter, my lids heavy. I'm worried about Chance and the puppy, Scarlett and Sebastian, and a dozen other things, but I'm too tired to figure them out right now. I need a good night's sleep and some time to talk with Chance.

I WAKE UP, ANXIOUS TO FIND CHANCE.

I trot over to his room, but he's already gone, his bed slept in but empty. I can smell the sweet cinnamon scent of the puppy in the sheets.

That means the puppy slept with him last night, bonding and marking her territory.

I track the scent down the hall until it mingles with the smell of eggs and toast. I step into the cafeteria, where scatterings of Puppio employees in blue T-shirts and lab coats are eating breakfast. In a far corner I see Chance and the Puppio finishing up a meal.

"We need to talk," I say.

Chance looks up, his expression neutral. I just reconnected with him after a whole year away, but he's looking at me like he doesn't know me.

"I can't really talk right now," Chance says. He lovingly scratches his new puppy under the chin.

That's one of my favorite spots.

"I'm worried about you," I say.

"Worried? What do you mean?"

"You and the puppy connected really fast."

"Are you jealous?"

"Of course not," I say, my face burning with shame. "I'm worried about the scar on your puppy."

"She doesn't have a scar."

"I saw something on her neck."

Chance shakes his head. "I don't have time for this. We're due for a training session. They're giving me lessons on how to work with Big Eyes."

"You already know how to work with dogs."

"Not this kind of dog," he says. "She's special."

The Puppio jumps from Chance's lap, yapping and ready to go.

"What about your mom? She must be wondering where you are."

"Dr. Pao called her, and they worked it out. She knows I'm safe and I'll be here for a little while."

Chance takes a sausage link from the plate and feeds it to Big Eyes. She attacks the sausage, tiny mouth nibbling it down to nothing.

I watch them, disturbed by what I'm witnessing. It's natural for a boy to love a new dog, but it's hard to get Chance's attention for more than a second right now.

The dog jumps up and down excitedly, and I scrunch up my nose from the apple pie scent.

"Can you smell the puppy?" I ask.

"I smell something delicious," he says, "but I don't really know what it is. Is that what you mean?"

"You don't smell apple pie?"

"Not exactly. It's more like—I don't know. It's a smell that makes me happy."

Very strange.

"We'll talk later, okay?" Chance says.

I stare at him, not knowing how I can get through to him. He starts to go and then he stops and looks back at me.

"What are you worried about, Wild? The time to worry was when we were out there with CAT chasing us. Now we're totally safe, and you're the one who's acting strange."

The Puppio takes off and Chance follows behind, jogging to keep up as if the dog were walking him instead of the reverse.

IT LOOKS LIKE ANY STREET IN SANTA MONICA.

There's a sidewalk lined with trees, a small cafe with tables out front, a Big Blue Bus bench on the corner. There's even a tall palm tree casting shadows from the lights above.

It looks like a real street in Santa Monica, but there's nothing real about it. It's a training area inside Puppio headquarters, a film set designed to replicate the look and feel of a street. Dr. Pao asked me to show the puppies how to defend their owners against an attack, and the stage has been set to make the training as realistic as possible.

Puppio employees pose as a middle-aged couple sitting at the table in front of the cafe, sipping iced coffee from mason jars. Three men walk down the sidewalk, chatting amicably, friends out for an afternoon stroll. I recognize one of them as a scientist I saw earlier, but he and the others are dressed in street clothes now.

Sebastian and Scarlett watch from a raised platform off

to the side. I make sure I have their attention and then I step into the scene.

"You'll walk down streets like this quite often with humans," I say. "Watch me and memorize what I do. Then I'll bring you down here and you can try it yourselves. You have to learn it first so you can teach the Puppio dogs later."

"Sounds good to me," Sebastian says.

"Most of the time when you're with your humans, there will be nothing to worry about, but sometimes there could be trouble. Some of the puppies will be given to people who need special protection, or people who live in dangerous places. They may walk into risky situations or come across people who want to harm their humans."

"How do you know who's dangerous and who's not?" Scarlett asks.

I step onto the sidewalk, and the three friends walk toward me, seemingly ignoring me. I sniff the air, detecting the mix of fear and adrenaline wafting from the pores of the men.

"Smell is your first defense," I tell Sebastian and Scarlett. "Humans can hide their intentions, but they can't hide their biochemistry."

Sebastian and Scarlett sniff the air.

"It smells a little musty," Sebastian says.

"Those men are sweating," I say. "Why would men be sweating on a cool day when they're not exercising?"

"I smell something else strange," Scarlett says. "Like seawater."

"Those are hormones that humans release when they're

under stress. They smell different than humans who are relaxed and happy," I tell her.

The friends separate, two of them continuing in my direction while the other crosses the street. The two men put their hands in their pockets, seemingly casual, but their shoulders are tense.

"Look at their posture," I say. "They seem like they're out for a walk, but the muscles around their shoulders and neck are straining."

"They're getting ready to attack you!" Sebastian says.

"That's right," I say. "They could be out to rob us, they could be kidnappers—"

"They could be from a rival dog company," Sebastian says.

"What do you know about that?" I ask.

"I've heard stories," Sebastian says. "Dr. Pao said there's a Russian company—"

"They're called CAT," Scarlett says. "Isn't that funny?"

They know about CAT!

"It could be CAT," I say. "What do you think CAT would do?"

"They could try to grab one of us," Sebastian says. "So they could do experiments."

I shiver as I think about being trapped on the plane, and the sound of the engine roaring as it took off—

"Be careful, Wild!" Scarlett shouts.

The men on the fake Santa Monica street rush toward me in a coordinated attack from multiple sides.

I snap into action. I leap from the sidewalk into the first man's chest, knocking him back into his friend. I whirl around at the man sneaking up behind me, and I snatch his pant leg, ripping it with my teeth and knocking him to the ground. He reaches for me, but I easily evade his grasp, and I turn my attention to the two men who have gotten their breath back.

They come at me, one on either side, trying to surround me in a pincer move. I slip between them, and leap toward the cafe table. The couple drinking iced coffee scream and scramble out of my way as their glasses crash to the ground. The table gives me some extra height, and as the first man comes toward me, I spring forward, paws hitting him on the shoulder and bouncing off, using my leverage to spin in the air and smash into his friend. He drops to the ground, out of commission.

The third man grabs a chair from the cafe table and runs at me, using it as a weapon. I bark at full volume and his eyes widen in fear. He swings too hard and loses his balance. I come up under him and smash my head into his groin. He doubles over, clutching his stomach in pain, then I use the advantage to kick him backward.

He trips on the edge of a curb and tumbles into the storefront behind him. But the wall is not stable—it's like a movie set, and the impact causes the anchor ropes to snap.

Without warning, a wood-and-brick wall is collapsing toward the platform where my puppies are watching. The platform tilts and gives way. Sebastian darts out from under the falling mass, but Scarlett is too close to get clear. She tumbles off the platform and howls in fear when she looks up and sees the heavy wall coming toward her.

I race forward at full speed. I make my body as low as possible, and I leap toward her. I want to snatch her and get us out of there, but there's no time, so I cover her body with my own. I brace in a crouch and take the full impact of the wall across my back. It's more than a hundred pounds of wood and brick, and it knocks the air out of me, and my legs start to buckle. I fight to stay on my knees, and I keep my back arched, making sure there's space for Scarlett under me.

The roar of the collapse is followed by silence and the smell of dust floating through the room.

I hear shouts around us as people begin digging under the rubble. I can feel heavy pieces being lifted away above me, and the weight slowly is relieved as they uncover us. It seems like it takes forever before I see light and feel the air on my back.

I stand and shake myself off, dust flying in every direction.

There's movement beneath me as Scarlett whimpers and stands up. She's disoriented and her eyes are unfocused.

"Are you okay?" I ask.

She looks up at me, blinking the dust off her long lashes.

"You saved me, Momma," she says, and her small tongue darts out and licks my cheek and lower lip, before she settles into the crook of my neck, crying and pushing herself against me.

I quickly check her for injuries. She appears unhurt, but she whimpers in fear. I tuck her under my chin and lean into her, letting my body warm and embrace her.

Technicians are shouting around us, calling for Dr. Pao and a medical team to check us out. Sebastian is looking on, concerned.

But I only focus on Scarlett, her body warm against me, her breathing in sync with mine. I think about the words she spoke, words that I've never heard.

You saved me, Momma.

I press my face into hers. "You're okay now, baby," I say, and I feel my heart open in a way it never has before.

THE REST OF THE DAY FLIES BY.

I take Scarlett for a medical checkup, and then I supervise an investigation of what went wrong in the training facility. At one point I ask Dr. Pao about Chance, and she assures me that his lessons with Big Eyes are going well.

It's almost dinner by the time I'm free, and I run down the hall to Chance's room, excited to see him and tell him what happened during the training session.

But when I push open his bedroom door, he's not there.

The room is perfectly clean, the bed stripped of its sheets.

Panic floods my thoughts. I bark and take off down the hall, racing along the scent trail of the Puppio dog that almost completely covers Chance's smell. I follow the two scents around one corner, then another, my speed increasing as I keep my head down and my senses on full alert.

I run past Puppio employees shouting as they're forced to jump out of my way.

The scent strengthens, which means I've almost caught up to them. I increase my speed, turn a final corner, and I stop dead in my tracks.

I'm in the front lobby of Puppio, just in time to see Chance at the door with Big Eyes by his side.

I look beyond him and see a Puppio van waiting in front of the facility, its engine idling.

"What's happening?" I ask, my voice shaky.

"Hi, Wild," Chance says, as calmly as if we'd bumped into each other in a dog park. "I was just heading out."

"Out for a walk?"

"For good. We're going home."

"We?"

He reaches down and gives Big Eyes a scratch on the head. "You know. Me and my puppy."

"Actually, I don't know. You're leaving and you weren't even going to say goodbye?"

"I wrote you a letter. It's on your dog bed. I guess you didn't go to your room yet."

"No, I didn't."

He commands Big Eyes to stay, and he walks over to meet me in the center of the lobby.

"I thought it would be easier if I wrote it down," he says. "I didn't want you to get upset."

I look at him, confused. "Upset that you're sneaking away? Why would that be upsetting?"

Chance bites at his lower lip. "You have a family now," he says. "You don't need me anymore."

"I just met those puppies," I say.

"But they're *your* puppies."

"That doesn't mean—"

"Doesn't mean what? That you won't be busy all the time being a mother to them? That you can spend time with them *and* me? I don't want to hear it, Wild. I saw it with my mom. Lots of promises and then—" He hesitates for a moment. "Wait, I know what you're doing. You're trying to guilt me into staying."

"Why would I try to make you feel guilty?"

"I don't know exactly, but I don't trust you right now."

I cry in pain at Chance's accusation. Before I can say anything else, Big Eyes comes over and does a little dance in front of Chance.

"She's super cute," he says with a laugh. "I can't resist her when she does that." Chance leans down and buries his face in the puppy's side. "She smells delicious."

"Not to me," I say.

Chance stops petting the Puppio and glares at me. "I'm leaving, Wild."

"Is that why your room is cleared out?"

He nods. "I have to go home. And let's be real—you have a home here."

I whimper involuntarily.

"There's no reason to be sad," Chance says. "We both got what we wanted."

"This doesn't sound like you."

"I disagree," he says. "It sounds like me—only happy. Maybe you haven't heard me happy before."

He pulls a leash out of his pocket and hooks it to Big Eyes. "She doesn't really need a leash. I mean, she's practically trained after only one day. But just in case. Dr. Pao says I have to keep her hidden for a few days until—" He pauses, looking over my shoulder.

"Until what?"

He doesn't respond. I turn and see Dr. Pao standing inside the room.

"Anyway, I have to get back to my mom. To school. To the soccer team."

"Do you have to go right now?" I ask, my voice high and cracking.

He nods. "That van's my ride."

Dr. Pao crosses past me and stands next to Chance. She puts a hand on his shoulder, and I grit my teeth.

"Come on, Chance," she says. "This is hard enough without dragging it out."

Chance takes out his earbud. I hear the transmission snap off, and with it, my only way of talking to him.

Chance drops the leash and runs back to me, dropping to his knees and flinging his arm around me.

"I love you, Wild. But you have your own life now. We both do."

I whimper and lick his face, trying to keep him there. He quickly opens my collar and replaces the earbud.

"Wait!" I shout, but he can't understand me anymore.

He releases his grip too fast and runs out the door.

I can only stand there, watching him go.

"I'll make sure he gets home safely," Dr. Pao says gently.

She follows him outside. I watch as he climbs into the van with Big Eyes. Dr. Pao closes the door, then walks around and gets into the front seat.

I close my eyes and howl in pain, the sound rising in pitch and echoing off the walls around me.

"WHAT ARE YOU THINKING ABOUT?" SCARLETT ASKS.

A few days have passed, and she and Sebastian are up on a climbing tree in the training gym. Sebastian is halfway up the structure, a series of platforms that leads to a revolving circle at the top. He's jumping from one platform to the next, struggling to make it to the very top.

But Scarlett left the tree without my noticing and she's standing in front of me.

"Why aren't you playing with your brother?" I ask her.

"You were whimpering," she says. "I heard you from across the room. Are you sad?"

"I was thinking about someone," I say.

"Chance."

I glance around, making sure we can't be overheard. "He was my friend. We took care of each other."

"What's it like to take care of a human?"

"It's nice," I say. "It feels natural. You take care of them, and they take care of you. That's the way it's supposed to be."

I lean forward to groom Scarlett, licking carefully around her head and ears while she moves closer and snuggles into my body. I breathe deeply, enjoying her puppy smell. She smells real, not like the Puppios.

"That tickles," she says when I lick her side.

Sebastian interrupts us with his barking. "Look at me, Scarlett! I'm the alpha dog!"

He's made it to the top of the apparatus, a whirling platform designed to test balance and challenge the puppies' climbing ability.

"Be right there," Scarlett shouts. "To knock you down."

"Come and get me!" Sebastian says, letting out a long, high puppy howl.

"You should go climb," I tell Scarlett.

"Will you tell me more about Chance sometime?"

"Sure."

"And also what it's like to live with humans?"

"Of course."

She starts toward the climbing tree, then turns back quickly. "You told me a secret, so I'm going to tell you one," she says, her voice low. She looks over her shoulder at Sebastian, making sure he's far away. "You need to be careful," she says urgently.

"Careful how?"

She comes forward, pretending to adjust my collar with

her teeth so she can whisper into my ear. "The things Dr. Pao says. Don't believe her."

"What things?"

"The reason we're here, it's not—"

"Come back, Scarlett!" Sebastian says. Sebastian's tone has changed. He's no longer asking her; he's demanding.

Scarlett presses her mouth up to my ear and speaks quickly. "You're in danger, Momma."

Before I can ask her what she means, a blur comes toward us from the climbing tree. It's Sebastian. He's sprung down from the platform, and he's racing across the floor, aiming like a missile at Scarlett.

She whips around and shouts angrily, "I told you I'd be there in a minute!"

But Sebastian doesn't stop. He hits Scarlett at full speed, knocking her away from me, the two of them tumbling across the floor.

The violence of the attack is surprising.

Is it possible he overheard her?

The puppies fight, snarling and nipping at each other. It might seem harmless if they were normal puppies, but these dogs get stronger every day, and this doesn't feel like a game.

"No fighting," I shout, but the siblings ignore me, snarling and rolling across the floor.

Sebastian tries to dominate her, two paws slapping down hard on Scarlett's face. Her head bounces off the floor with a crack.

"Sebastian! Scarlett!"

I shout their names, surprised by this new role. I sound like one of those humans in the park who gets upset when their dog runs off the leash.

I move to intervene just as Sebastian grabs Scarlett by the fur and shakes her hard.

"Enough!" I shout, but Sebastian won't listen.

I can see Scarlett is rattled, and I slap at Sebastian with a paw to the hindquarters, not hard enough to hurt him, but with enough strength to startle him into releasing his jaws.

Scarlett pulls away, and her collar snaps and goes skittering across the floor. She's in shock from the fight, and she stands alone, startled and unmoving.

I call to her, and her eyes begin to focus, and she realizes her collar is missing.

She scampers across the room, running to retrieve it. As she passes by, I see an ugly surgical scar on the back of her neck, deep enough that fur has grown in abnormally in the spot.

It's the same scar I saw on the Puppio puppy.

She drops down and rolls over her collar. It attaches automatically to her neck, sealing itself with a magnetic click. With the collar back in place, she stands up and shakes herself off.

"What was that all about?" I ask.

"Just playing," Sebastian says with a smile.

They trot past me as if nothing happened, and they start to play on the climbing tree.

"Is that true?" I ask Scarlett.

"Just playing," she shouts, and she jumps on the apparatus like nothing happened.

I smile like everything is fine, but I'm thinking of the scar I just saw and the hastily whispered things she said to me before Sebastian's attack.

I LOOK FOR DR. PAO BEFORE THE NEXT DAY'S TRAINING SESSION.

I tap at her office door, and she motions me inside.

"How are you bonding with your puppies?" she asks.

I think about the scar I saw under Scarlett's collar. I want to ask Dr. Pao about it, but I have to choose my words carefully.

"We're still getting to know each other," I say. "Their schedule is packed. I'd like more time for us to play. It's important if they're going to get along with humans."

"I wish I could give you more time, but I don't have any to give. The first fifty dogs are going out this weekend."

"You're releasing the Puppios?"

"We're holding an adoption event at STAPLES Center. The dogs are going to the mayor, the governor, a few celebrities, studio heads, some YouTubers."

"VIPs and influencers."

"What better way to get the message out?" the doctor says. "Fifty dogs this weekend, five thousand dogs by the end of the year. That's why we've been working Sebastian and Scarlett so hard. I want them to be able to support these dogs when they're in homes."

"Support them how?"

"Monthly training workshops. Puppy school for owners and dogs. That kind of thing."

The idea of weekend workshops with Puppio trainers and dogs working with new owners makes sense, but something is still bothering me.

"Scarlett's collar fell off earlier," I say.

The doctor hesitates. "They're growing quickly," she says. "We need to work on that collar."

"It's not about the collar design," I say. "I saw something on her neck."

"You saw the surgical scar," Dr. Pao says matter-of-factly. "I imagine that was disturbing for you."

I flash back to the time I found a scar on my own body and pulled a BreedX microchip out of my thigh. The memory makes me shiver.

"Why did they have surgery?" I ask.

"Remember I was the one who created the BreedX technology that was stolen by General Rupani. I had the chips and I decided to use them."

She comes over and sits on the edge of the desk in front of me, so we're close in the small office.

"These Puppios are ultra-sophisticated dogs, the first of

a new breed. Cars have VIN numbers, computers have serial numbers, and my dogs have ID and tracking chips."

"These are live animals. They're not property."

"They're our creations, and we need to be able to monitor them. Sebastian and Scarlett will help us. You were out there, so you got a sense of what CAT was trying to do."

CAT. It's the first time I've heard Dr. Pao mention them.

"What's CAT all about?" I ask.

"They're a group of bio-hackers trying to beat us to market."

"I thought they were Russian?"

"Not officially. They were thrown out of Russia, and now they're in exile, people without a country. If they can get their hands on our tech, they can impress their government and maybe get back home. These dogs are priceless to them."

"That's why they were trying to capture me."

"And Chance, so they'd have control of you."

I imagine Chance at home alone with the Puppio.

"I know what you're thinking," Dr. Pao says. "We're keeping track of him. Big Eyes has a chip so we can track their movements at all times. Trust me when I say he's safer with us than he could ever be with you."

I whimper, the comment hitting a little too close to home.

"It's not personal," she says. "It's a resource thing. We have a whole staff who can look after him. He only had you."

She goes back around her desk and sits down. "You're suspicious. I'd be worried if you weren't. But you're one of the family now. No more secrets between us. Agreed?"

"Agreed," I say.

She leans forward and looks into my eyes. "You want to protect your pups. I think that's a good sign."

"A sign of what?"

"That you're becoming a real mom," she says, and she touches her chest, directly over the heart.

I DREAM OF CHANCE.

I'm giving him a tour of Puppio headquarters, showing him all the things I've learned about the facility since he's been gone.

"I want to meet the puppies," Chance says.

"But you have a Puppio now," I say.

"I lost her," he says. "I want to get another one."

He sounds different in the dream, his voice too loud so it echoes off the walls around us.

A door slides open and a gaggle of Puppios come tumbling out and rush toward Chance. I smell the overly sweet scent of multiple puppies, and the odor is nauseating to me.

Chance squeals in delight, but before he can open his mouth to speak, the Puppios leap on him. It seems like they want to play, but the game becomes real and it turns into an attack. The tiny puppy bites are savage, small mouths digging into Chance's flesh.

"Stop!" I scream, but the dogs won't obey me.

I turn to find Sebastian standing nearby, smiling and looking on as the Puppios attack Chance.

"Help him," I beg.

"You taught us how to fight," Sebastian says. "You taught us everything we know."

He leaps into the pile, snarling and baring his teeth as he goes for Chance's neck.

I wake up from the dream howling in terror, my breath coming in gasps. I can still hear Chance's screams echoing in my head.

I hop out of bed and shake my head violently, trying to get the feeling of the dream away from me.

Now that I'm awake, I realize what's been bothering me about my puppies.

The scars on their necks, Scarlett's warning, the whole idea of dogs training other dogs.

Training them to do what exactly?

I decide to talk to Scarlett right now, in the middle of the night, away from Dr. Pao or the Puppio employees who are around all the time. I want to examine her scar more closely and ask her some questions to find out exactly what she knows about Dr. Pao's plan for the Puppios this weekend. I head for the room where she and Sebastian sleep, hoping I can wake her up without his knowing and find someplace to talk to her alone.

BUT WHEN I GET TO THE ROOM, THE PUPPIES ARE GONE.

I stand in the doorway of their sleeping area, expecting to see them in their dog beds, but there's no one here. Their blankets are cool, and the scent is not fresh. Which means they haven't been to sleep yet.

Where could they be in the middle of the night?

I trot down to the cafeteria, but there's no sign of them.

I sniff my way through the dark hallways. The air in the Puppio facility is highly filtered, but the puppies' odor is so familiar to me now, I can track it with only a few molecules in the air.

I follow their scent through the hall and down a stairwell, all the way to a basement area where I've never been.

Why are the puppies in the basement at night?

I follow the scent around several corners, passing a furnace room and a maintenance storage area.

The scent dead-ends in the corner of the basement against

a solid wall. I back up to see if I've made a mistake, but the trail again goes to the same place.

A solid wall.

I examine it more closely, and I find that it's not as solid as it looks. There's a small crack running along the baseboard. I press at it, and I hear a swishing sound.

A dog-size door opens—a secret door embedded into the wall, tucked away in a place where nobody could find it.

Nobody, that is, except the puppies who already know where it is.

I cautiously walk through the door and find myself in a long, low tunnel. The air is cool and moist, suggesting that I'm underground. I follow the tunnel for about a hundred yards before it starts to ascend upward. I'm wondering if I'm in an exhaust vent of some kind, and I imagine myself popping up in a field somewhere outside headquarters.

I soon reach the end of the tunnel, and I push through another doggy door.

I look around, disoriented. I'm not outside; I'm in an entirely different building.

Unlike Puppio headquarters, this structure is windowless, the walls thick and the doors reinforced. Scarlett's and Sebastian's scents are instantly diffused, lost in a tsunami of other odors.

I hear voices ahead of me along with the barking of dozens of dogs. I follow the sounds, walking up a steep flight of stairs, then pushing my way through a door at the very top.

I'm on a platform high above a huge room filled with computers and tech equipment.

Two stories below, I see Sebastian and Scarlett standing near a group of scientists in white lab coats. Across from them is a large dog pen filled with four dozen Puppio puppies. It smells like a food court, and my senses are overwhelmed by a dizzying combination of odors because of the number of animals.

The Puppios bark and jump at one another inside the pen, their energy agitated from being so close together.

Meanwhile, Sebastian and Scarlett look on calmly from the side.

A woman in a business suit steps out from the group of white-jacketed individuals. I recognize her posture immediately, the bow-legged walk and intense energy.

"Sebastian, you're up first," Dr. Pao says.

So much for not keeping secrets from each other.

She leans over and adjusts Sebastian's collar.

"We're ready to begin the experiment," she says to an operator on the other side of the machine. "Scarlett, you can relax. Let's see how Sebastian does this time."

"Stand back and watch how an expert does it," Sebastian says, and Scarlett grumbles.

"Activate the chips," Dr. Pao says.

An assistant flips a button on the machine, and Sebastian's collar starts to glow red. As if on cue, the Puppios begin to whine in their pen.

I see a red glow emanating from the back of the Puppio dogs' necks, burning brightly through their skin. Four dozen puppies with four dozen red dots, all of them glowing the same color as Sebastian's collar.

Sebastian's collar turns green, and one by one, the chips on the puppies' necks shift to green.

"Connection initiated," Dr. Pao says.

Sebastian barks, and the Puppios immediately stop fighting.

"Awesome," Sebastian says.

"Try moving them," Dr. Pao says.

I see the tension on Sebastian's face as his collar throbs with green light. The Puppios begin to organize themselves, moving like soldiers into three neat lines inside the pen.

"It's working," Dr. Pao says.

Sebastian barks with effort as he sends another command. He's not talking to the Puppios, at least not in human language. But his commands are somehow being transmitted to their chips.

Dr. Pao lied to me. These are not just tracking and communication chips. They allow Scarlett and Sebastian to control the Puppio dogs.

Control them for what?

"I've got an idea," Sebastian says. "Watch this."

The Puppios stand up on hind legs, four dozen of them at the same time, hopping like puppets and prancing back and forth.

"Stop showing off," Scarlett says.

"Why? It's fun!" Sebastian says.

"That's enough," Dr. Pao warns. "It's not a game."

Sebastian grunts with effort, and the Puppios drop back to all fours, standing like normal dogs again.

"Sorry about that," Sebastian says, lowering his head submissively. "I couldn't resist."

Dr. Pao looks at him scoldingly. "We expect you to maintain military discipline in this facility."

I don't do military compounds, Junebug said when we first arrived.

She was right about this place. It's a military facility.

Scarlett and Sebastian are the communication links in some kind of plot to control the Puppio puppies.

"The communication works well with four dozen dogs," Dr. Pao says. "But what's our current capacity?"

"We can scale almost indefinitely once we boost the signal," one of the scientists says. "Four dozen, four thousand, or more. Sebastian and Scarlett will control every dog within range of the collar if that's what you want. After that, we'll run into physical interference from buildings and whatnot."

"We'll need to breed more master puppies," Dr. Pao says.

"Seems that way," the scientist says.

"It shouldn't be a problem now that we have Wild back."

I gasp and it feels like the floor drops out from under me.

Sebastian and Scarlett don't just train the dogs. *They control them.*

Dr. Pao signals with her hand, and the machine is turned off. The glow fades on the puppies' necks, and Sebastian's collar goes back to normal.

One of the Puppios lets out a howl. It's quickly picked up by the other puppies.

"What's happening?" Dr. Pao asks.

The dogs sniff the air, howling, and they begin to crane their necks, looking up.

Toward me.

My scent has alerted the Puppios. Sebastian raises a paw, pointing into the air toward where I'm standing.

"It's Wild!" Scarlett shouts.

"Come down, Momma," Sebastian calls to me. He beckons with his head, tail wagging, inviting me to join them as if nothing unusual were going on.

I look at Scarlett. She shakes her head ever so slightly, tail tight between her legs, her posture warning me away.

Sebastian is calling me down, and Scarlett is telling me to get away.

"How did you get in here?" Dr. Pao calls up to me.

Dr. Pao shouts orders, and a group of blue-uniformed employees rush forward. They are not wearing the T-shirts with the friendly Puppio logo on them. These are rugged soldiers' uniforms designed to protect the wearer during a fight.

One instinct would have me rush down and grab my puppies and bring them with me. But when I see Dr. Pao whispering orders to the Puppio soldiers, another instinct kicks in.

One that tells me I should escape.

The soldiers fan out across the floor, making their way to the stairs that lead up to where I'm standing.

I'm torn, not wanting to stay, but not wanting to leave Sebastian and Scarlett.

"I want to talk to you about this," Dr. Pao shouts.

Scarlett begins to whimper in high, panting tones. Sebastian growls and snaps at her, and her breath catches in her throat.

Dr. Pao starts walking toward the stairs below, following the soldiers. "Please wait for us," she calls to me.

The soldiers are at the bottom of the stairs. The first of them begin to climb, their boots vibrating through the metal steps below me.

"Let me explain, Wild," Dr. Pao says.

But I don't wait.

I RUN.

I scramble across the scaffolding, down the stairs, and back through the tunnel between buildings. Two buildings. Puppio headquarters and a Puppio military research facility.

By the time I get to Puppio headquarters, a piercing alarm is sounding in the halls.

I race through the building, moving toward the front exit so I can get away. What I'm not expecting is the building to turn against me.

I've barely made it halfway to the reception area when the door locks snap and the lights go off, plunging the building into darkness.

A thick gas is released through the ventilation ducts. At first, I fear I'm being poisoned, and then I sniff and smell a dozen dogs and people that weren't here a second ago. The gas is some kind of scent scrambler, sending false odors through the facility to confuse me. The building must have been designed to prevent the Puppio dogs from escaping. Now the defenses are being used against me.

Without being able to trust my vision or sense of smell, my mind spins like a compass needle. I hit a wall and bounce off, run forward and hit another one. I stop in the middle of the hall, confused.

Pull yourself together, girl!

I hold my breath and close my eyes, giving up smell and vision. Instead I use the map in my head rather than my senses. I feel my way forward, touching doorways with my snout, matching them to my memories to locate my position in the building.

My sleep quarters, the training gym, Dr. Pao's office, the computer storage room. I see them in my head and I keep moving, staying low and trusting myself. I hear security officers, but I don't react to them, knowing they're at as much of a disadvantage as I am in the dark and gas-filled space.

Eventually, I sense the room widen around me, and the scent thins. I open my eyes and find myself in the reception area. I make out the large windows that face out to the parking lot. I try the front door, but it's locked.

I move back several feet and take a running start. I lower my head and pivot, hitting with my shoulders and the side of my body, hurtling through the glass like a cannonball, smashing and rolling on the asphalt. My eyes snap open, and I'm already in motion, running through the grass, breathing deep, the night air fresh and crisp in my lungs.

There's a high fence up ahead, and beyond it—freedom.

"Stop, Wild."

I turn back and see Dr. Pao. She's alone, standing about twenty feet behind me.

"I knew you would be able to escape," she says. "Even with the building's anti-dog defenses."

A growl rumbles in my throat. I look out past the fence. The road beyond Puppio is quiet, which means I'll have a head start to get away from the soldiers.

"Security will be here shortly," Dr. Pao says. "We only have a moment."

"I want Sebastian and Scarlett," I say.

"They don't belong to you."

"They're my puppies."

"Puppies. Not property."

I hear security officers moving through the building toward us. I turn back to the fence.

"If you leave, you're never going to see them again," Dr. Pao says.

I hesitate, at least until I think of Chance out there with a Puppio dog. I have to find him and get him away from that dog. I crouch, preparing to leap the fence.

"Please don't do this, Wild. The boy has his own life now, and your life is here with us."

Glass breaks in the lobby as the security officers force their way through the windows.

I snarl, baring my teeth at Dr. Pao. "You hated General Rupani," I say. "You hated everything about him and Maelstrom, and now you've become just like them."

"That's the story you're telling yourself," she says. "It's not the truth."

"Goodbye, Doctor."

I leap the fence, landing safely on the other side.

"I can't let you walk away from Puppio," she says. "There's too much at stake."

I look through the wire mesh at the security officers streaming into the parking lot. I hear the high-pitched scream of zappers charging. I look back, surprised to see the baton-like weapons that were a part of the Maelstrom arsenal, their tips crackling with electricity. The familiar sound fills me with terror.

"I'm not going to let you go," Dr. Pao says.

"Try to stop me," I say.

The zappers fire, lightning arcing through the sky toward me. But I'm already in motion, racing away so fast that the bolts crash down behind me, exploding into empty space. I hear the vans starting up behind me, engines roaring and men shouting as they prepare to give chase.

I RUN FOR HALF A MILE, MY SENSES ON HIGH ALERT.

I pause and listen behind me, expecting to hear a throng of soldiers in Puppio vehicles chasing me.

But there's only silence.

I stand in an empty field and turn into the wind, letting the air wash across my nose, tracking the scents for a mile or more in all directions.

No diesel fuel, no odor of humans.

But I sense something else. I stare ahead and I see a pair of eyes watching me from the darkness, two red orbs unblinking in the tall grass.

The Finisher!

The sight of those eyes sends a shiver down my back.

Could he be working for Puppio? For Maelstrom?

"What do you want?" I shout to make my voice heard over the wind. "Why are you following me?"

The eyes disappear, then reappear in a different spot.

I growl and move through the grass, rushing forward, ready to fight him once and for all.

I race toward the eyes, but as soon as I get close to them, they disappear.

I stop, disoriented. I look around to try to locate him, but he's nowhere to be found. I think my mind is playing tricks on me, but then I examine the grass at my feet. The blades are tramped down and broken, and there's a single, large paw print in the soft earth.

The Finisher was here.

I don't have time to try and figure out why or where he might have gone. Instead I remember the sight of Sebastian controlling the Puppio puppies through his collar. I don't know what Dr. Pao is planning once the Puppios are released, but I know that Chance has one and he's in danger.

I have to get to his apartment as fast as I can.

THE STREET IS QUIET AS I APPROACH.

No police, no Animal Control vans.

The streetlights are on, so I stay in the shadows, moving toward Chance's apartment undetected. I walk through the parking lot and around the complex, fighting the desire to rush up the stairs and burst into Chance's living room.

Nothing seems out of place, so I go up the back stairs, where Chance's bedroom window is lit up. I climb up on my forepaws and crane my neck to peek in. Chance is at his desk with his schoolbooks open in front of him. The Puppio dog Big Eyes is by his side, napping peacefully.

I don't want to startle him, and I don't want his mother to be alarmed, so I tap my nails against the window.

Chance turns and sees me. The Puppio puppy stirs but doesn't wake up. He cracks open the window. "What are you doing here?" he whispers.

I'm a little startled by his reaction. I thought I'd be

welcomed back at first sight, but there's something in his expression and tone of voice that I don't understand.

I huff and turn my collar to him so he can take out the earbud.

He hesitates and looks back at Big Eyes. The Puppio scent hits me, and I scrunch up my nose.

"I don't think I should let you in," Chance says.

I plead with my eyes, and Chance relents and puts in the earbud.

"I need to talk to you," I say. "You're in danger."

"From what?" he says curiously.

"Can I come in for a minute? It's not safe out here."

"Is this some kind of trick?" he says.

"What are you talking about?"

"I thought you were living at Puppio headquarters now. I thought you had a family."

"I had to leave—"

"Leave your family?"

"Let me in," I say, frustrated. "Why are you being so weird?"

"I'm not the one who's sneaking around in the middle of the night."

"Please, Chance."

He glances behind him to make sure the door is closed and Big Eyes is sleeping.

"Come in but please be quiet. I don't want my mother to know you're here." He pushes the window and slides open the screen.

I leap from the back stairs through the window in one motion, landing silently on the floor inside his room.

Big Eyes snaps awake and growls high and threatening despite her tiny size.

"Big Eyes!" Chance shouts, and the growl stops. She rushes to Chance's side, taking up guard by his leg. Chance reaches down and lovingly strokes her, giving special attention to her ears and the top of her head. "She loves the ears thing," he says.

I look at Chance and the puppy, and I can feel the bond that has cemented between them. "I have news about the Puppio dogs," I say.

"Let me guess. They're bad and I have to get away from them."

"Yes! But if you knew that—"

"I knew *you'd* say it. Or something like it."

"What do you mean?"

"You're jealous, and you've been jealous from the moment I met Big Eyes. I figured you'd come up with some story to try and break us apart."

I'm stunned by what I'm hearing. Chance hasn't moved away from Big Eyes. The puppy is still rubbing against his leg and looking innocent.

"The Puppio dogs can be controlled by Sebastian and Scarlett. They're like some kind of dog army."

"Army to do what?"

"I have no idea, but Dr. Pao is planning to release the first puppies in a few days, and we have to stop her."

"You don't want kids to have great dogs like Big Eyes?"

"You're not hearing me, Chance."

He takes a deep breath and holds it like someone losing

his patience. I'm afraid he's not going to talk to me, but then words start to spill out.

"Do you remember last year after we defeated General Rupani? You had a chance to come and live with me and Mom, but you walked away."

"Because it wasn't safe—"

"You were gone a year, Wild. A whole year. For the first month I thought you would change your mind. Then, after we moved, I'd leave the window open at night because I was worried you wouldn't be able to find my scent. My mom would yell for me to shut the window because the air conditioner was on, but when she closed it, I'd slip out of bed and open it again."

"Why didn't you tell me this earlier?"

"Because we were a little busy running from Russian hackers. And because it was dumb, and I didn't want to talk about it."

"It's not dumb," I say softly.

He turns to me, his lower lip trembling. "Dogs don't leave. They're supposed to be loyal."

I whimper involuntarily, his words scaring me.

"Dogs don't leave, but you left," he says. "You were gone so long I wondered if I'd imagined the whole thing. I mean, a talking dog? That's crazy, right? I thought maybe it was a stage I went through, like a kid who believes in the tooth fairy until he gets older and finds out the truth."

"I'm sorry I hurt you, Chance."

I take a step toward him, but he holds up a hand to stop me.

"I'm not a kid anymore," he says. "I'm fourteen now, and I've got a dog who loves me and who's loyal." He opens his arms and Big Eyes leaps onto his chest with a delighted bark.

"I'm your best friend," I say, "and I'm loyal."

"*You're* loyal?" He sneers. "I don't think so, Wild."

He flips open the laptop on his desk.

There's a twenty-four-hour news station on his browser, and it features a close-up picture of me with a giant headline in red:

BLOODTHIRSTY DOG ATTACK ON SANTA MONICA STREET

I rear back on my paws, stunned by what I'm seeing.

"You once told me you'd done bad things in the past, and I didn't believe you," Chance says. "Well, guess what? I believe you now."

He clicks the screen, and I watch a video of myself running in slow motion as I attack the Puppio employees in the training room the other day. The room was nothing more than a movie set designed to look like a Santa Monica street for the training exercise, but it doesn't look like a movie set on the news.

It looks real.

I see myself running down the street, tackling one person after another, kicking them to the floor, roaring with fangs bared and spittle flying from my lips—

The man comes at me with a chair over his head like he did in the training exercise, and I slam his midsection and he doubles over in pain. I turn to the camera snarling, and the video freezes on my face. A wild dog. A dangerous animal attacking multiple people.

The video doesn't show the end of the exercise when the wall collapsed. It doesn't show how it fell, or how I dove beneath it to save Scarlett from being crushed.

It looks like a video of a dog on a rampage.

"That video is a lie," I tell Chance. "It didn't happen like that."

"It looks like you lost it and started attacking people," Chance says. "They're screaming and trying to get away from you."

"It was a training exercise. Dr. Pao must have filmed it so she could use the video against me."

"That's not what she told me."

"You spoke to her?"

"She called to say you'd gone crazy and hurt a lot of people. Then you'd broken out of Puppio. She was afraid you'd come back here and try to hurt me—or Big Eyes. And here you are. First you betrayed Maelstrom, which I understood because they did terrible things. But then you betrayed me last year by leaving. And now you've betrayed Puppio and your own children."

I look at Big Eyes, watching me from Chance's arms with a contented expression on her face. I don't know how much she can understand, and I don't know if her chip is sending a feed so Dr. Pao can watch us right now.

I want to snatch her from Chance's arms and explain everything to him. But if I touch her, he'll hate me forever.

I take a panting breath, and I make my voice calm. "Those things you're saying about me, Chance—they're not true."

"It's not you in the video?"

"It's me, but it's not the whole story."

Chance isn't listening anymore. He's scrolling through an online social media platform, whipping through my image hundreds of times over. The training exercise has become a viral video of a vicious dog attack.

"Listen to me," I beg him. "Puppio is like Maelstrom with a new name. Dr. Pao is no better than General Rupani."

"You blame Maelstrom for everything," Chance says, "but I don't think it's about them. Maybe you're confused. Or maybe you're a bad dog like they say on the news. I don't know what to believe."

"Believe me."

He bites at his lower lip and studies my face.

"Please, Chance."

But his expression is cold as he shakes his head.

I hear police sirens outside the apartment, coming closer. Big Eyes mimics the sound with a high warble.

I look out the window and see patrol cars pulling up in the parking lot.

"The police found me! But how—"

"They didn't find you," Chance says. "I called them."

"What?"

He takes out his earbud and reaches toward my collar, releasing the secret port and popping it back before I can stop him.

The bedroom door flies open and Animal Control officers rush into Chance's bedroom, backed up by police officers. I bark at Chance, warning him. Big Eyes yelps, agitated by all the chaos in the room.

"Take it easy, girl," Chance says quietly. "These officers are here to help you."

The Animal Control officer points at me. "Are you talking to her?" he asks Chance.

"It calms her down when she hears my voice," he says.

"Whatever," the officer says. "Keep talking." He steps toward me with a noose on a pole.

"Stay calm, girl," Chance says as if he's talking to a different dog. A dangerous dog.

"Yes, girl," the officer says. "Just relax and nobody will get hurt."

I rear back, going into a defensive crouch, ready for action.

Suddenly, a Taser hits me, the electric shock passing down my spine and through my nerves. My muscles contract and release in rapid succession, freezing me in place.

I try to get up, only to be hit with another blast of electricity. I grit my teeth trying to stay alert, but it's too intense, and I black out.

When I wake up, a noose is already around my neck, followed quickly by another noose, the two of them holding me firmly in place.

Another shock and I lose my balance and go down.

A final shock, and I'm on the ground and twitching, the image in front of me flickering as if in a dream. I see Chance looking down at me, his face cold. Animal Control officers hover over me, putting restraints on my legs and a muzzle over my head.

I think about Sebastian making the Puppio puppies follow his commands.

I think about the Finisher, his eyes glowing red in the night.

"I trusted you," I hear Chance say.

A needle goes under my skin. It burns when the injection goes in and the tranquilizer enters my bloodstream.

My eyes roll back into my head. I try to steady them, to lock my gaze on Chance, to let him know I don't blame him, to tell him everything is going to be okay.

"How did you know she'd come back here?" the Animal Control officer asks Chance.

"She used to be my dog," Chance says, cradling Big Eyes in his arms. "But I have a new puppy now."

The room begins to spin, and then everything goes black.

I SMELL DOGS.

Their scent fills this place. It's embedded in the walls and floor, the odor so thick it's like a blanket suffocating me.

I open my eyes, still groggy from the injection.

I'm alone in a reinforced cage, a bowl of water in front of me, the bowl welded to the floor so it cannot be moved.

The last few hours come rushing back to me.

The Puppio revelation, seeing Chance, the news report of me attacking the soldiers, the Animal Control officers overwhelming me in Chance's bedroom.

Why did Chance betray me like that?

I can almost smell the sweetness of the Puppio, and I remember something Dr. Pao said when Chance first met the Puppio puppy:

They've bonded. It's as easy as pairing your iPhone.

There's something about the scent that bonds humans to the dog, something more than just smelling like delicious food.

Pain surges through my skull, and I sit up, blinking hard and trying to clear my head. It's hard to think right now, much less put the pieces of the puzzle together.

How long have I been out?

A muzzle is locked over my jaws with a small opening for my tongue. I look down at the bowl of water. It looks stale and it's cloudy with sediment. Not appealing under normal circumstances, but my throat is so dry, I don't have a choice.

I bury my snout in the water, lapping at the bowl. The water has a chemical tinge, and I realize too late that it's drugged.

A breeze tickles my neck. I reach up with a paw and feel that my collar is gone, replaced by a neck restraint connected to the muzzle. That collar is my access to the world of humans. Without it I'm lost.

A wave of despair hits me as I think of Sebastian and Scarlett.

I wonder if they're okay, and if they know why Dr. Pao has given them the power to control the Puppio puppies.

You have to get out of here, girl.

I look around the room. There are cages around me, all of them empty, yet the scent of dogs lingers. Dogs that were afraid.

I hear movement in a corner. A cage far from my own.

I'm not alone.

I see a large gray pit bull lying on its side, panting. It wears a muzzle, just like me.

The door flies open, and I smell humans. The pit bull barks wildly.

A young man in a white lab coat comes into view, heading for the pit bull's cage, followed by an older man, who guides him with hand signals.

"Thatta boy," the young technician says to the pit bull as he reaches into the cage and hooks into a hinge on the dog's muzzle. He drags it out of the cage as it barks in confusion.

There's nothing I can do to help this dog right now, so I stay quiet, my eyes closed, not wanting the men to know I'm awake until I understand more about where I am.

"What about that one?" the young technician says. "We should check on her."

"I'm not going near that cage without protection."

"She's just a dog."

"Really? Did you see that attack video?"

The young technician takes a breath. "I saw it. But she didn't look dangerous when they brought her in."

"A grizzly bear doesn't look dangerous until you're in its mouth. And I want to get home to my family tonight if that's okay with you."

I open my mouth to howl at them to leave the pit bull alone, but a wave of dizziness comes over me, and I flop to the cage floor, the drug still in my system, and I fall asleep again.

THE MEN ARE HERE AGAIN.

Their voices pull me up from a drugged sleep. I squint and find myself in a clinical white room. I'm on a large metal table with a frame structure bolted to its sides. My neck is clipped into the frame, holding me tight.

"I hate this stuff," the young technician says as he crosses in front of me.

"You saw what she did."

"The whole world saw it."

"Let's get this over with," the older guy says. "Turn on the TV or something. Distract yourself."

The older guy goes to a cabinet and removes two vials and syringes. He places them on a tray while the young technician looks for the remote control.

I look at the syringes, and I shiver on the cold table.

I think of Chance's angry words.

Dogs don't leave. You're supposed to be loyal.

191

But I wasn't loyal. Not to Chance, not to my puppies, not even to Maelstrom.

I shake my head, trying to organize my thoughts through the fuzz in my brain.

Is Chance right? Maybe I am a bad dog, not in the way the video shows, but in a different way that's even worse.

The young technician finds the TV remote and flips it on.

I see a video of several dozen puppies in a pen at Puppio headquarters. The Puppio dogs have huge eyes with long lashes, and they prance on all fours and yip at the camera.

The reporter says, "There have been a lot of less-than-pleasant stories about dogs lately, so we thought our viewers might enjoy something hopeful. A new technology company has created the dogs of the future...today."

The Puppios wiggle their ears, tongues lolling out of their mouths as they cock their heads this way and that. Even without smelling them, humans will experience them as the perfect puppy.

Behind them, I see Sebastian and Scarlett, and my stomach clenches.

"These little Muppets are more than they appear," the reporter says. "They can keep your family safe crossing the street, dial nine-one-one if there's a break-in, and even detect if your kids have been using drugs. I hope they don't mind if Mom and Dad have a cocktail after a long day at work."

The female anchor laughs. "In my house, they'd be detecting a lot of white wine."

I look across the room. The older guy fills the first syringe and places it on the tray, his face somber.

"You'll have to wait a year or more to get ahold of one of these puppies," the reporter says. "The first batch cost more than a hundred thousand dollars, and they're going to be delivered to an elite clientele—CEOs, celebrities, and politicians—at a live event at STAPLES Center in downtown Los Angeles tomorrow."

"My daughter would love one," the anchor says.

"Puppio promises there will be more affordable dogs in the future. Their dream is to have a Puppio in every home."

"Wouldn't that be nice?" the anchor says.

The two technicians come toward me with the tray.

If I do nothing, Dr. Pao will release the puppies into the world.

But what can I do now? I've lost Chance, and my image is on every screen in Los Angeles. The whole city thinks I'm a monster.

That's when I realize why Dr. Pao didn't chase me herself. She warned me that she couldn't let me walk away. Instead of coming after me and risking Puppio's reputation, she's destroyed my opportunity to live a normal life with Chance.

Maybe it's time for me to surrender and let this happen. I've lost, Dr. Pao has won, and the world is going to have to take care of itself.

The technicians put the tray next to me. I lie down, readying myself for what's to come.

What about Chance?

My conscience nags at me.

What about your puppies? Maybe you can get them away from the doctor?

The young technician glances at the TV. "Cute puppies," he says.

"All puppies are cute," his colleague says. "It's when they grow up the problems start."

Maybe I'm never going to have a normal life, but don't Chance and my puppies deserve one?

"Sorry, girl," the young technician says. "This will all be over soon."

"No, it won't," I say, rising to all fours, a growl vibrating in my chest.

"Hurry up!" the older guy says, realizing I'm fully awake. I jerk my neck violently and snap the frame that holds me to the table.

Chance deserves a life. My puppies deserve a life. And Dr. Pao has to be stopped.

The men jump back, startled at my sudden burst of strength. I kick the medical tray to the floor, then I use a paw to whip off my muzzle.

"Grab her!" the older guy says, lurching into action. The young technician reaches for the syringe on the floor, and I pivot off my front legs and send him careening into the wall.

The older guy is running for a cabinet with a warning sign on it: LIVE WEAPONS. I race after him, vaulting over the table and smashing his head into the side of the cabinet before he can get it open. He groans and goes down, unconscious.

I look back at the young technician. He's slumped on the ground, wide-eyed, staring at me.

"P-please don't hurt me," he stammers.

I see the terror in his eyes. This young guy was just doing his job, but I don't like his job. Not one bit.

I get in his face and howl with rage, teeth bared and inches from his throat. He screams and passes out.

I leave him there, and I speed across the room, crashing through the door and out into the hall.

I hear someone shouting my name, and the door on the far side of the hall pops open.

Junebug and I are facing each other in the middle of the hall.

She blinks in surprise. "I came to save you. But it looks like you saved yourself."

"I'm really happy to see you!" I say, tail wagging.

She rushes forward and gives me a big hug. Then she points to a black bud in her ear. "It's my old Maelstrom earbud. I dusted it off and it still works. But I can't understand you." She looks at my neck. "Where's your collar?"

Great question, I think.

I take off and she follows. We run through the shelter together, and I hop up to look into the windows of the rooms I pass.

I find what I'm looking for near the rear of the building. A storage room with a large rolling garbage bin piled high with collars. I grasp it with my front paws and knock it over, spilling the contents across the floor.

The scents of dozens of dogs washes over me at the same time. But there's only one collar I'm seeking, its odor distinct from the others.

Mine.

I snatch it from the pile, lie across the floor, and spin, feeling the magnets click as it snaps into place.

"Is it working?" I ask.

Junebug smiles wide. "Loud and clear," she says.

"Aren't you afraid of me?"

"Why would I be afraid?"

"The video on TV."

"You think I'm going to believe anything Puppio releases? A kindergartner with a phone could make a better deepfake than that."

A yelp in delight, rubbing myself against her.

"Dr. Pao is responsible for all of this, isn't she?" Junebug asks.

I nod.

"I told you it was a military compound," she says, hands on her hips.

"You were so right."

She looks behind me. I turn and see the dozens of collars spread across the floor. "All those dogs," she says quietly.

I hear barking in the distance. "Come with me," I say.

We run through the building until we find the dog holding area. Junebug and I open the cages of the stray dogs who are imprisoned here. Junebug leads the pack and me through the halls until we find the rear entrance, the door lock smashed, a crowbar on the floor where she left it when she broke in.

I kick open the doors, and the dogs run free. I watch them scatter in the night, silently wishing them well.

"What now?" Junebug says.

"The news said Puppio is delivering the dogs to downtown Los Angeles tomorrow. We have to be ready."

"Ready for what?"

"To squash the plan."

"Cool," she says. "Sounds like my kind of action."

"But first we have to save Chance."

"Let's hurry up on that one. He keeps sending me videos of him and that stupid Puppio dog. I can't take it anymore." She motions for me to follow. The Mercedes is parked around the corner. "I know where Gregory keeps the keys," she says, and she flings open the driver's door, making room for me to dive in first. Then she hops in and starts the car.

I think about the time she saved Chance and me at the PetStar last year, crashing through a line of Animal Control officers and pulling up like a professional race car driver.

"Are you sure you remember how to drive?" I ask her.

"You're joking, right?" She pumps the gas, making the engine roar. "I promise this is going to be fun," she says.

The tires squeal as we take off together to find Chance.

THE CAR IDLES AS
WE WAIT.

We're hidden around the corner from Chance's apartment complex. Eventually, Chance's apartment door opens, and he runs down the stairs with Big Eyes by his side. Once they hit the ground, Chance takes wide steps, and Big Eyes runs between his legs in a figure eight, so fast and precise she looks like a trained circus dog.

"What's going on with that puppy?" Junebug asks.

"It's a Puppio," I say. "Super smart, pre-trained—"

"And really cute."

"She's okay."

"I mean *mega* cute," Junebug interrupts. "She's like a cartoon character come to life. They're going to sell a million of those things."

"Chance hasn't been the same since he met her."

She glances at me. "You're sensitive about this, huh?"

"More like concerned," I say.

Chance starts toward the mailbox, but halfway there he

drops to his knees and wrestles with the puppy, covering it in kisses.

"Whoa, I see what you mean," Junebug says. "He's being weird, even for Chance."

"I'm afraid they're going to be hard to separate," I say.

"We'll see," Junebug says, and she puts the car in gear and rolls through the parking lot and stops in front of Chance.

He jumps back, startled, and the puppy yips with concern. "What are you guys doing here?" he asks.

Junebug jumps out of the car. "You mean how did we get Wild out of dog prison? Because that's where you put her, you know."

"I didn't put her anywhere," Chance says.

"You called the police on her," she says.

"Because she's dangerous."

"She's not dangerous."

"Did you see the videos?"

I hop out of the car and stand between Chance and Junebug.

"The old Chance wouldn't have believed that video for a second," Junebug says.

"What do you mean, 'the old Chance'?"

"Wild thinks the puppy is making you behave differently."

"She's just jealous because I've got a puppy and I'm moving on with my life."

Junebug looks at me, astonished.

"Tell him to put in the earbud," I say.

"Wild wants to talk to you," she says.

"Well, I don't want to talk to her," Chance says.

Chance picks up the puppy, cradling her in the crook of his arm. The puppy settles in, front paws on either side of its head as it yawns.

"Can you smell that?" I ask Junebug.

She sniffs. "Sure. It smells like apple pie. That's really weird."

"Does it make you want to take the puppy home with you?"

"Not really. I'm more of a chocolate-chip-cookie girl."

"Are you talking about my dog again?" Chance asks angrily.

"You don't think it's weird that your puppy smells like dessert?" Junebug asks.

"So what? Dr. Pao said every puppy smells like the owner's favorite food."

"Wild's worried about you. And so am I."

"There's no reason to be worried," Chance says. "I'm happy. Maybe you can't deal with that."

A squeal of tires cuts through the silence. My head snaps up, and I can just make out a Puppio van far down the street.

"What do you see?" Junebug asks.

The van accelerates hard, racing toward us. The puppy starts to howl, a loud, warbling sound like a siren.

"What's going on?" Chance asks. "Why's she making that sound?"

I look at Big Eyes and I see the faint glow on the back of her neck. Her chip is being activated.

"We have to go," I shout to Junebug. "They're controlling the puppy from the van."

"The van is talking to your dog," Junebug tells Chance. "Drop that thing and let's get out of here."

The dog grabs tightly to Chance's arm. "I'm not leaving my dog," he says firmly.

Junebug pulls out her keys. "Good luck, then, you stubborn jerk."

"Hey, that's mean!" Chance says.

The van is down the street, nearly on top of us.

"Hurry!" Junebug shouts to me, and she runs for the car.

I look at Chance clutching on to the puppy. I can't talk to him, can't explain anything—I look at the van barreling toward us.

I can't leave him here.

I dive between Chance's legs, startling him, and I spin around and grab him by the back of his belt.

"Whoa!"

I pull him backward toward the car. He loses his balance and stumbles, releasing the puppy, who hops to the ground, yelping furiously.

Chance is disoriented, so I haul him into the back seat before he realizes what's happening.

"Step on it!" I shout to Junebug, and she jams the gas. The rear door swings closed as the car rockets forward, just in time to avoid the Puppio van that screeches to a stop behind us.

"Where are we going?" Chance shouts.

"STAPLES Center," Junebug says.

"You can't take me against my will," Chance says, regaining his breath. "It's kidnapping."

"You told me you weren't a kid," Junebug says.

Chance scowls.

"We're just getting you away from that puppy," Junebug says, "then we can have a mature conversation."

"No way. Not interested," Chance says.

He kneels on the seat, his face pressed to the rear window, looking for his dog.

"Big Eyes!" Chance shouts.

The puppy is running after us, tiny legs going as fast as they can.

"That thing is tenacious," I say.

Junebug looks in the rearview mirror. "It's fast!"

"She loves me," Chance says. "She doesn't want to let me go."

Junebug rolls her eyes and speeds up.

The Puppio van pulls around the corner behind us. It quickly catches up to Big Eyes and stops. The back doors fly open, and I see Sebastian jump out of the van and gather up Big Eyes by the scruff of her neck and jump into the van with her.

I look back and see the Puppio van take the same corner. It stops, unsure which way we went. Then it turns in the wrong direction and continues at speed.

"We lost them," I tell Junebug.

She nods but doesn't slow down, weaving through the traffic around us, making sure we're safe before she lets up on the gas.

"My dog!" Chance shouts. "Take me back to her."

"Listen to yourself," Junebug says.

I watch the two of them arguing, and I smell the lingering odor of the puppy where it marked Chance with its scent.

I notice a gas station ahead with an attached car wash. "Pull into that station."

Junebug gives me a quick, curious look in the mirror.

"We need the car wash," I tell her.

"Where are we going?" Chance demands. "I don't have time for this."

He still can't understand me since he refused to put in an earbud.

"I guess Wild wants us to wash the car."

"A car wash? Now?"

Junebug pulls up to the entrance and pays for the wash. The front tires slip onto the track mechanism and pull the car into the tunnel. The spray nozzles turn toward us and the first jets of soapy water shoot at the car from every direction.

"This is going to take forever," Chance says, exasperated.

"I think it's going to go faster than you think," I say.

And I open the door and pull him out of the car, directly into the soapy spray.

THE WATER HITS US FULL IN THE FACE.

Chance sputters and tries to get away, but I grasp his pant leg and hold him tight, keeping the two of us in the stream of soap and water.

"You're trying to drown me!" he shouts, but some soap gets in his mouth, and he spits and coughs, no longer able to talk. I move as the car moves, following it along the track while keeping a firm grip on Chance.

It seems like it takes forever before the soap jets retract, replaced by rinse bars that spray down like a horizontal shower. The water flows and drenches us. I can feel Chance shivering but unharmed in my jaws.

The rinse cycle comes to an end, and I hear the roar of hot air heading for us. Chance looks up, frightened by the noise.

Enough is enough, I think, and I open the car door, push Chance inside, and dive in after him, biting for the door handle and slamming it closed behind us as the hot air blasts the car.

Junebug looks back at us, wide-eyed.

Chance shakes water out of his hair. I sniff up and down his body. The puppy scent is gone, replaced by the odor of lemony car wash soap. I lick at his face, letting my warm tongue bring him back to the present moment.

The car wash tunnels ends. Junebug slips the car into drive and pulls out of the tunnel and parks by the vacuums.

Chance blinks hard as he looks at us. I lean over and expose my collar to him. To my relief, he presses on it and slips in the earbud.

"How do you feel?" I ask.

"I'm okay," he says, his voice thin. He squeezes water from his hair, and he sits up suddenly energized. "Why did you do that?!"

"I had to wash the puppy scent off you."

He shakes water from his hair. He looks from Junebug to me and his expression softens.

"The Puppio marked you the first day you met," I say. "You've smelled like her ever since."

"Don't all dogs mark their territory?" Chance asks.

"This is next level," I say. "You were closely bonded to the specific dog."

"Bonded? It was more like superglued," Junebug says.

"I still miss her," Chance says. "It's just not as powerful as it was before."

"I think the smell is only one part of the bonding process.

It's like you bond with the dog emotionally, and the scent turns up the volume."

"Why did Dr. Pao make them that way?" Junebug asks.

"Puppio isn't what it seems," I say. "People are going to bond to the dogs. And the dogs have chips installed in their necks that allow them to be controlled from a central communication point."

"Controlled by who?" Chance asks.

I think of Sebastian making the dogs sit up and beg at Puppio.

"I'm still putting the pieces together," I say, not wanting to talk about what I saw my puppies do until I better understand what's happening.

"Are you sure you're okay?" Junebug asks Chance.

"Would you stop asking me that question? You're worse than my mother."

"He's back to his normal self," Junebug says with an eye roll.

"What was all that stuff you were saying about STAPLES Center earlier?" Chance asks.

"There's a Puppio event today. The first set of puppies are going to be adopted by the public."

"We have to stop it," Junebug says. She turns to Chance. "Do you want to come?"

"Why wouldn't I?"

"Because you were obsessed with that puppy."

"It's funny, but the longer I'm away from her, the less attached I feel."

"I think that's how they're designed," I say. "Do you think you'll be okay at the Puppio event?"

"If I can help you stop Dr. Pao, then count me in," Chance says.

Junebug grins from ear to ear, and I bark in excitement as she accelerates out of the gas station, heading for downtown LA.

MEDIA TRUCKS ARE LINED UP OUTSIDE STAPLES CENTER.

The sun glints off the dramatic green glass curves of the arena, temporarily blinding me. I squint and squeeze deeper into the wheel well of a large truck parked across the street.

Junebug and Chance are nearby, crouching down as we watch the lucky families and invited guests walk the red carpet into the arena, interviewed by the media and clutching gold-embossed invitations in their hands.

Only a single arena entrance is open, tightly controlled by security officers in dark suits. Around them are smiling young people in bright blue Puppio T-shirts, their backs adorned with the company logo and a new catchphrase: *Puppio. The future starts now.*

We have to find a way into the facility, yet there are hundreds of people around who could recognize me from yesterday's news story.

"Stay here for a second," I tell Chance and Junebug, and

then I belly-crawl beneath the truck, moving to get a better angle on the arena. I notice a row of vehicles parked around the side. One of them is a cargo van, its back open and over-flowing with boxes. I see T-shirts printed with the words FUTURE PUPPIO OWNER. It's some kind of promotional item they're giving away to spread the word.

I spring back to Chance and Junebug. "Give me one minute, then walk straight toward that door on the side of the arena."

"You can't go out there," Chance says. "People will recognize you."

"I have an idea," I say. I nuzzle the back of his hand, and then I take off.

I use the parked cars as cover, and I dart across the street and run up to the van, snagging a shirt in my teeth and taking it into the alley nearby. I slip my front paws through the T-shirt and roll it up over my back.

Now instead of hiding, I prance out into the middle of the crowd, the Future Puppio Owner T-shirt covering my coat, my head on swivel like a happy, proud dog out for a walk.

Chance and Junebug are nervously crossing the street, and I fall in by their side.

"Smile and keep walking," I say.

We pass a group of Puppio employees. I feel Chance tighten up next to me. I jump in front of him, taking the lead.

"How cute!" one of the employees squeals as I pass by. I let out a quick bark and toss my head in the air. That earns me a burst of giggles from the employees.

"It's almost like she knows where she's going," Junebug says, following behind me.

She and Chance wave to the employees, and the three of us keep walking, right past the security people, who laugh and wave, and through the busy service entrance into STAPLES Center.

THE BACK OF THE ARENA IS A MAZE OF HALLWAYS.

We get away from the Puppio employees, following the hall until it opens into a larger area with passageways going in multiple directions.

"What now?" Chance asks.

"I have to find Dr. Pao. She's the key to all of this," I say.

"If those puppies get out into public, everyone will want one," Junebug says.

"We have to warn people," Chance says.

Junebug looks up and down the hallways. "I think we should separate," she says.

"Bad idea," I say.

"This place is massive, Wild. We'll never find her. Besides, you can run much faster than us. If you smell her, you'll start chasing her, and we won't be able to keep up."

"If we separate and you find her, what happens then?" I ask.

"We fall back and we call you," Chance says. "We don't do anything stupid."

Junebug nods dramatically.

I don't like this plan at all, but I think they're right. STAPLES Center has endless hiding places, and I can move much faster than they can.

"You and Chance stay together."

"I'm not letting him out of my sight," Junebug says.

"Maybe I'm not letting *you* out of *my* sight," Chance says.

"Just take care of each other," I say.

"Will do," Chance says. He throws me a thumbs-up, then he and Junebug take off down the hall.

I want to yelp and go after them, but I stop myself. The best thing I can do is find Dr. Pao first while we still have the element of surprise.

I sniff deep and listen closely, exploring the space by scent and hearing. The smell of fresh-baked pastries lingers in the air around me. The Puppios must be nearby, waiting to be transferred to their new owners.

I start down the largest hallway, moving in the opposite direction from the puppies' scent. I'm trying to think like Dr. Pao. I'm guessing she'll be somewhere up high watching from a vantage point where she's safe and in control. I take the stairs away from the arena floor and head toward the VIP suites. I sniff my way down the hall, eventually picking up her scent at the top of the stairs. I track it down the hall, passing a series of A-level suites until I get to one at the very end.

The door is unguarded, which gives me pause, but I sniff at the crack under the door. Dr. Pao's signature is unmistakable. I ready myself for anything, then I hop up and use my paw to open the door.

DR. PAO IS ALONE, LOOKING AT THE ARENA BELOW.

I'm in a beautifully decorated suite with plush leather seats and a wall of windows overlooking the arena stage. I can hear the crowd noise piped into the room through speakers.

Dr. Pao glances back as if she's been expecting me. "Impressive turnout," she says. "Just as I hoped, the Puppio puppies are irresistible."

I glance at a set of video monitors above her head, different perspectives on the stage adorned with Puppio banners. Multiple cameras are set up to stream the event live to cable channels and news.

"Do you want to join me?" Dr. Pao asks.

"I can see just fine from here," I say cautiously. I look at the crowd gathering below. Movie stars and their families are in the audience waiting to see the Puppio dogs in real life for the first time. I recognize the mayor and a California senator chatting with a group of dignitaries. I scan the VIPs and invited guests taking their places in the front row. Behind them, the news media is set up in a long line of cameras and microphones.

"Almost time to begin," Dr. Pao says. She turns toward me and puts her hand on the table next to her.

There's a zapper baton there, inches from her outstretched fingers.

"That's a Maelstrom weapon," I say, pointing at the zapper.

"*Was* a Maelstrom weapon. I own their equipment now."

I growl, plotting the paths that will get me close enough to strike at her. I expect her to reach for the weapon, but instead she crosses her arms and smiles at me.

"I know you're angry," she says, "but it's tough to take you seriously when you're wearing a T-shirt with our company logo."

I look down at the FUTURE PUPPIO OWNER T-shirt, and I tear at it with my teeth, ripping it from my body.

"That was unnecessary," Dr. Pao says scoldingly.

I search the room, looking for hidden traps. It's a small room, and I'm sure there's nobody here but the two of us.

Why is Dr. Pao so calm?

"I was expecting you, Wild. I heard you escaped from the Animal Control facility earlier, and I knew you couldn't stay away," Dr. Pao says.

"I thought this state had no-kill shelters."

"True. They only put down the most dangerous animals. The ones who can't be rehabilitated."

"Regardless, I'm not in the shelter anymore, am I?"

She smiles. "You getting out didn't surprise me. The surprising part was how you got in. Evidently, the boy called the authorities. It sounds like he betrayed you."

My face burns with shame. "It wasn't a betrayal. He saw the video you released."

"*Killer dog on the loose*. Very effective, wasn't it? People love a good animal attack video. It instantly went viral."

"It can't be good for your dog adoption event."

"Actually, it's the opposite. It helped us today. Nobody wants to think about a big, scary dog grabbing their children, but everyone loves a puppy." She looks down at the crowd waiting expectantly in the arena.

"I'm not going to let you release those puppies," I say.

"You might want to glance at the monitor on the wall behind you before you make demands."

I turn to see what she's looking at. The screen behind me doesn't show a view of the arena like the other screens.

It's a live video feed of Chance and Junebug.

They're tied to chairs in the middle of an empty room with cement walls. Chance's expression is determined, but I can sense his fear from the way he holds his shoulders tight. Junebug is next to him, scowling at the camera.

"They didn't get far before we caught them," the doctor says. "I'm holding them somewhere under the arena. Let me tell you, it's quite a maze down there. I got lost three or four times today, and I had a map."

I look at the video feed of the kids, memorizing every detail of the room where they're being kept. I sniff the air in the VIP suite, trying to detect a trace that might lead me to him.

"You're trying to smell him, but it's not going to work. I asked my people to lay false scent trails through the arena. They're walking the halls right now rubbing his jacket on various corners. I imagine it would take you hours to follow all of the false trails and find the boy."

A shadow crosses Chance's face in the monitor, and a man and woman step into the frame next to him. Puppio soldiers in blue uniforms.

Chance sneers at the soldiers. His courage makes my heart swell, but he's still just a boy, and he looks small next to the adult soldiers.

"They can see us just as we see them," Dr. Pao says. She nods to a small camera mounted in the corner ceiling.

"Chance!" I shout, but he doesn't look up.

"No sound," she says.

Which means there's no way for me to communicate with him or Junebug.

"What do you want with them?" I ask.

"It's not them. It's you, Wild."

Before she can say any more, an image of a Puppio puppy appears on every screen in the arena. Massive eyes, long eyelashes, shortened snout that curls up on the sides to give the puppy an appearance of smiling.

The audience explodes with expressions of "Awwww" and shouts of "They're so cute!"

"They can't resist the Puppios," Dr. Pao says, delighted

with herself. "Even Chance fell in love with a puppy. His bond with that dog was so strong, he forgot all about you."

"He didn't forget. The smell on those dogs is like a drug."

"That's a part of it. You're right. The dogs bond chemically, emotionally, and psychologically with their humans. People will fall in love and stay in love. That's my gift to the world—a dog who never gets taken for granted, never gets forgotten, and never becomes a burden. Normal dogs can't compete. They'll be out on the street in no time. Just like you were."

I back up, tail between my legs.

"Tough to hear the truth, isn't it?"

"The plan is to bring designer puppies into the world?"

Dr. Pao pulls on her suit jacket and fixes her hair.

"Once the world sees my dogs in real life, they won't be able to resist. I already have a waiting list with five thousand names on it, families desperate to pay a hundred thousand dollars for a puppy. I can't breed dogs fast enough to keep up with demand."

"What do Scarlett and Sebastian have to do with it?"

"The puppies behave independently unless their chips are activated. Then Scarlett and Sebastian have direct control over them. You saw for yourself. I can make thousands of dogs sit at the same time. Isn't that cool?"

I shake my head. "It sounds like a power trip."

"You still don't get it, do you? The dogs control the children, and I control the dogs."

My mind races as I sort the repercussions of what she's saying. "That's why you need Sebastian and Scarlett."

"Exactly."

A Puppio dog in every home in the city, each of them controlled by Sebastian and Scarlett. Dr. Pao will be a modern-day Pied Piper with access to every family, their secrets and vulnerabilities, and their children.

"What would you give to the woman who controlled your children?" Dr. Pao asks.

"You'd give her whatever she wanted," I say quietly.

She smiles wide and spreads her arms to indicate the crowd below. "Money. Power. Respect. Everything General Rupani stole from me."

"Why are you telling me this?"

"Because I want you back, Wild."

"After everything that's happened?"

"I can't afford to hold grudges. Sebastian and Scarlett need you. If you come back, you have my word that Chance will go free."

I look at the stage in the arena. I see Sebastian and Scarlett standing off to the side, watching as the arrangements are completed before the event begins.

"We'll make sure Chance has money for private school, then college. When he's old enough, we'll arrange for him to get a great job. We'll take as much pressure as we can off him and his mom. They've struggled enough, don't you agree?"

I look at Chance and Junebug on the monitors, the soldiers looming over them.

I think about what Dr. Pao is offering. A sacrifice.

My life for Chance's life.

"You said Chance would go free. What about Junebug?" I ask.

Dr. Pao's face goes dark. "That's another matter. You know where the girl comes from."

"She hasn't seen her father in over a year. General Rupani is gone, and Maelstrom along with him. You said so yourself."

"I can't have her free and out in the world. It's too dangerous to us."

"Then what's going to happen to her?"

"Why are you worrying about her?" Dr. Pao asks. "After what her father did to you?"

"What *he* did. She tried to help me."

"She's her father's daughter," Dr. Pao says with a scowl. "She's not your concern. It's the boy, right? It's always been about the boy for you."

Chance and Junebug squirm in their seats on the screen.

I stare at Dr. Pao. "You'd sacrifice a girl to launch Puppio?"

"For Puppio? I'd sacrifice a girl, a boy—even a dog."

Applause starts in the arena below, rising to a thunderous chant. "Pup-pi-o! Pup-pi-o!"

A grin spreads across Dr. Pao's face. "It's time for me to go. And it's time for you to make a decision."

She motions toward the door, and a half dozen Puppio soldiers come into the room, blocking my exit.

"You say you hate General Rupani, but you've become just like him."

The screen on the arena floor lights up, and the crowd goes quiet.

Puppio. The Future Begins Now.

"I'm better than he ever was," Dr. Pao says. "Now, are you coming with me or not?"

"I'm coming with you," I say.

She nods and her shoulders visibly relax. "You're a smart dog, Wild. You're going to make a great member of the team."

"I'm coming with you," I say, "but I'm not part of the team."

"What are you talking about?" she asks, but before she can get the rest of the words out, I leap at her from across the room, smashing against her chest and sending the two of us sprawling backward.

We hit the plate glass window with a loud crack. It gives way, and suddenly we're hurtling through the air, falling together toward the arena stage below.

THE CROWD SCREAMS AS WE TUMBLE TO THE FLOOR.

Broken glass cascades down like rain. We hit a pile of boxes, Puppio shirts and hoodies flying into the area around us as Puppio dogs scurry out of the way. The employees onstage duck and cover, avoiding the glass shattering on the floor around them.

The audience screams, first because they're stunned by a woman and a dog falling out of the sky, but then because they recognize me.

"It's the dog from the TV!" a woman shouts.

Dr. Pao moans and rolls over, struggling to her feet. "Stay calm, everyone," she says. "I have this under control."

The Puppio officials quickly clear the stage, leading people to safety.

Dr. Pao turns to me, rubbing her head. "What have you done?"

I growl and ready my leap. But before I can take action, the Puppio dogs surge forward, four dozen of them at the same time, filling the gap between the doctor and me. They crouch in a protective stance and a low rumble vibrates in their throats. Their cuteness is menacing when multiplied several dozen times over.

I notice Sebastian standing to the side, his body rigid, his face tight with concentration. The green glow on his collar matches the green on the puppies' necks.

Sebastian is controlling the Puppios.

Dr. Pao looks at the panicked crowd being ushered out of the arena and the Puppio employees rushing around chaotically.

"You ruined the launch event," she says accusingly.

"You expected me to do nothing while you try to take over the city?"

"I expected you to choose the boy over yourself."

My stomach clenches and a howl catches in my throat as I think of Chance and Junebug alone against Puppio soldiers.

"It's too late for the kids now," Dr. Pao says. "It's too late for you, too. No more deals, no more opportunities. I want you out of my life."

I glance behind me and see that most of the crowd is gone, but the news media is transfixed, cameras pointed toward the stage.

"Protect!" Dr. Pao shouts to Sebastian and Scarlett.

The Puppio dogs surge toward me in a wave, barking in unison. I crouch, not wanting to hurt the dogs, but afraid I won't have a choice.

"What about the cameras?" I tell Dr. Pao. "If the puppies attack, everyone will see what they can do."

"You mean that they're capable of protecting a human against a predator? I want everyone to see that."

For some reason the dogs stop in place, and I sense confusion down the line. The puppies start up again, take three steps toward me, and stop.

I look over and see Scarlett concentrating hard, her collar glowing red.

Scarlett is giving them different commands than her brother.

"Cut it out!" Sebastian shouts at her. He nips at her hindquarters, and she yelps and backs away, her concentration broken.

The puppies surge forward again, their necks glowing green, but then they turn red and stop.

It's a power struggle between Sebastian and Scarlett, the two of them fighting over whether they want the puppies to attack or retreat.

"Stop blocking me!" Sebastian tells her.

"It's not a fair fight," Scarlett says. "There's only one of her and there are so many of us."

"I'm not here to fight," I tell them.

"Why are you here?" Scarlett asks.

"To save Chance and Junebug. And to take you away from Puppio."

"Don't listen to her," Dr. Pao says. "You saw what she did. She tried to kill me."

"We're a family," I tell my dogs.

Sebastian shakes his head. "Puppio is our family."

The Puppio dogs jerk forward, reconnected to Sebastian's command. I crouch and growl, ready to defend myself.

Dr. Pao rushes into the center of the puppies. "STOP!" she demands. "Sebastian and Scarlett! Take the puppies away with you."

"What about Wild?" Sebastian says.

"I'll take care of her."

Sebastian starts to retreat, but Scarlett stops him.

"We can't leave Wild alone," she says. "She's our mother."

Sebastian hesitates, looking from me to Dr. Pao. Then he takes a step toward the doctor.

"You have free will," I tell them. "You can make your own decision."

"There's no free will," Sebastian says. "There's only loyalty."

Scarlett looks at him, confused.

"We're soldiers," he tells her forcefully. "We take orders, remember?"

"I remember," she says sadly. She glances back at me, her expression pained.

The Puppio dogs rush from the stage all at once, racing in every direction to get away from me.

"Don't go," I say.

Scarlett gives me one final look, then she turns and follows her brother offstage.

I have no choice but to watch them go, my lips tight, shoulders hunched in grief.

Dr. Pao smiles thinly. "It looks like you lost everything

you care about," she says. "That's what happens when you make bad choices. You end up alone."

"Maybe so," I say. "But now we're both alone."

I roar and start toward her, readying my attack. A flicker of worry causes me to hesitate.

Why would Dr. Pao risk standing alone against me when she knows how strong I am?

She quickly grabs a baton from the table and flicks it open. The baton extends outward and electricity crackles from the end.

A zapper.

She wields the Maelstrom weapon like an expert. The high-pitched tone sounds as the zapper charges. I howl in pain and rear back on my hind legs.

"There are witnesses everywhere," I say.

"That's the whole point," Dr. Pao says quietly. "As far as they know, the violent dog from the TV just pushed me through a window, and now she's loose onstage. When I destroy her, I'll be a hero."

She raises the zapper, preparing to fire.

I think about the scene from the media's perspective, and I realize she's right. It will look like she saved the puppies by taking on the dog everyone is afraid of.

I howl in pain and frustration and charge toward her. Dr. Pao brings up the zapper, sparks flying from its tip. There's little chance I can get to her before the lightning bolt hits me, but if I can dodge at the right time, I might be able to avoid it.

She presses the trigger as I prepare to leap—

And nothing happens.

"What?" She looks at the zapper, surprised and horrified.

"My camera's not working!" one of the media people shouts.

"What happened to the signal?!" another one calls out.

Dr. Pao looks around frantically. "Something's blocking the electronics in the room," she says.

I hear a shout as the rear doors burst open, and a group of hooded figures run into the room, racing toward the stage.

"Dr. Pao!" a man with an Eastern European accent shouts.

It's the Uber driver!

He leaps onto the stage along with the men from the plane and several additional people I've never seen before.

"CAT," Dr. Pao says with a sneer.

The CAT people form a line as they move toward Dr. Pao.

The Uber driver comes close, and I tense, ready to defend myself.

He gives me a quick look, then walks right past me.

"We don't need you anymore," the Uber driver says. "We have something better."

His men rush toward Dr. Pao, and I see the first man pull a can of knockout spray from his hoodie.

They're trying to kidnap Dr. Pao!

If they capture the doctor, they'll have the secrets of Puppio directly from the woman who created it. I can't let that technology get into the hands of a Russian hacking group.

I growl and race toward them, intent on breaking up the group and pulling Dr. Pao away so I can deal with her myself.

But the Uber driver is one step ahead of me. He spins

around, pulling a small electronic device from his pocket at the same time. Before I can react, he clicks a button, and the lights go out, plunging the arena into darkness.

I jump toward their last position, but I make contact with nothing but empty air.

The lights snap on, and I twist this way and that, desperate to find the doctor.

But I'm alone on the stage.

Dr. Pao is gone.

I run forward, tracking her scent as it mingles with the men from CAT. I sniff all around the floor where they were a moment ago, but I only smell a chemical agent masking the scent.

Did they capture the doctor? There's no way to know.

CAT is gone, and Dr. Pao with them.

It looks like you lost everything you care about, Dr. Pao said.

Chance and Junebug! I have to find them.

I RACE THROUGH THE HALLS, FRANTICALLY SEARCHING FOR THE KIDS.

The main lights are off all over the building, but the emergency power has kicked on and the hallway glows red. I leap down the stairs two at a time, heading for the tunnels under the arena, ignoring the many scent trails of Chance that Dr. Pao placed to confuse me. Instead I set my focus on Junebug's scent, using her to track down Chance.

I run up and down the hall, peering through the dim light and pushing open doors, desperate to find them. I move faster and faster, the frustration growing inside me. I hear a dog howling nearby, its calls echoing off the acoustic tiles. Its voice is familiar; the dog is me. I'm howling with grief and rage, howling as the adrenaline from the confrontation with Dr. Pao wears off.

I check all the doors in the hall, but I still don't find the kids. Desperation overwhelms me, and I stop in the middle of the hall, not knowing which way to turn or what to do next. I roll and mash my snout into my forepaws, crying in frustration.

I cry for the boy I fear I've lost, and for my puppies, who walked away from me.

A voice snaps me to attention.

"Wild!"

It's Chance, calling my name. I sprint around the corner and stop.

Chance is at the top of the stairs looking down at me.

"You're okay!" he shouts.

I scurry up to him, sniffing at his legs and whining, amazed that he's here and he's unharmed.

"I'm sorry I couldn't get to you in time," I say. "I had to try and stop Dr. Pao."

"You don't have to explain. We heard everything she said in the room."

"Not everything. CAT is here, too."

"What happened to the lights?"

"It was some kind of electromagnetic pulse. CAT knocked out the media signals, the zapper weapons, and then the electricity in the entire building."

"That's not good."

"We'd better get out of here. Where's Junebug?"

"She's getting the car."

People shout from below, the last remnants of the audience clearing out of the arena as the police rush in.

"Let's have our reunion outside where it's safer," I say.

"Deal," he says, and we jog next to each other, moving

in the opposite direction from the crowd, heading toward the rear of STAPLES Center.

"How did you get away from the soldiers?" I ask him.

"I did what you taught me," he says. "I let them under-estimate me."

"When did I teach you that?"

"Remember you told me how people look at you and they just see a normal dog? Well, I look like a normal kid, right? So I cried and said I had to go to the bathroom. One of the soldiers felt sorry for me. She untied me and didn't watch me closely. That's when I grabbed the zapper baton off her belt. They didn't think I knew how to use it. But I learned last year when we were fighting Maelstrom."

"You zapped a soldier?" I ask, amazed.

"Two soldiers. So I guess it was a double zap," he says proudly. "Then I untied Junebug. I'd say those soldiers learned not to underestimate a kid."

I laugh in delight, and Chance guides me to a large room with an Exit sign in the corner. The sound of a siren passes by on the street outside.

"I was so worried about you," I say.

I whimper, and Chance runs a hand across my head and over my ears, reassuring me. "You don't have to worry so much," he says. "I'm not a little kid anymore."

"That's obvious."

"Now let's get out of here." He opens the door and we step outside.

JUNEBUG IS IN A CAR ACROSS THE STREET, ENGINE RUNNING.

There are sirens in front of STAPLES Center where police cars are pulling up, but it's strangely quiet on the side street.

Junebug rolls down the window of her aunt's Mercedes. "Let's get out of here before the cops arrive!" she shouts to us.

"The cops are the least of our problems," Chance says.

"What are you talking about?"

"Wild says CAT is back."

"They're not looking for us," I say.

I consider going after Dr. Pao, but when I look at the kids, I realize that will have to wait. I have to get everyone home safely before I can even think about CAT again.

We start to cross the street, and a flicker of movement catches my eye from a nearby alley.

I let out a short bark, stopping Chance in his tracks.

"What is it?"

He barely gets the words out before an animal darts out of the alley, moving so fast it's a blur. It whips up the sidewalk and stops in front of us.

I instinctively step in front of Chance, guarding him with my body.

The Finisher is blocking our path, panting heavily, watching us with half-closed eyes.

I remember his big paws and the strange mix of breeds in his features. He's like a Siberian husky with the snout and jowls of a bloodhound.

But the dog I remember was powerful and thick with muscle. This version of the Finisher is thinner, and his face is skin and bones.

"It's true, then," I say. "Maelstrom still exists."

"Maelstrom?" He looks confused.

"Isn't that why you're here? You've been following me. I saw you at the soccer field where Chance was playing."

"Yes," he says, his voice a breathy whisper.

"You were behind the apartment building the other night, too."

"I've been following you. But not for Maelstrom."

"Why, then?"

"I need to talk to you, She-Nine."

He calls me by my laboratory name, the name Maelstrom assigned me when I was a soldier dog.

"I go by Wild," I say.

"*Wild*. I'm sorry. I remember now."

I feel Chance shift behind me. He's gaining courage, and he stands by my side, defiant.

The Finisher laughs, a deep choking sound. "The boy loves you."

"Don't worry about the boy," I say. "This is between us."

I tense, preparing for anything. But the Finisher's posture is subdued, his head low, tail down. He doesn't look like a dog who is about to attack.

"I need to ask you something, Wild." He lowers his head and shivers like a Chihuahua. That's when I realize he's sick. "Have you heard from Maelstrom?" he whispers.

"You work for Maelstrom," I say. "Why are you asking me?"

"I tried to contact the general. I tried to find him, but I couldn't. It's been a year now, maybe longer. It's hard to keep track of time. I'm so tired." He steps forward and stumbles, catching his balance before falling.

"I'll get him some water," Chance says, and he takes off for the car.

I expect the Finisher to chase him, but he doesn't move, eyes locked on mine. I step forward, lowering my guard.

"Where have you been living?" I ask gently.

"On the streets, in the forest, scavenging. I'm not cute like you, Wild. Nobody is going to adopt a dog that looks like four different dogs stitched together in the lab."

Chance runs back with a bottle of water. "Is it okay to give it to him?" he asks.

"Put it down and back away," I tell him.

He pops the cap and places the bottle on the ground. The Finisher darts forward and knocks it over, lapping furiously.

Chance gives me a worried glance.

"Wait in the car," I tell him.

"I don't want to leave you."

"I need a minute alone with him."

Chance reluctantly crosses back to the car.

"I haven't heard from Maelstrom either," I admit. "I heard General Rupani is gone."

"That would explain it," the Finisher says.

"But I don't understand—if you're not working for Maelstrom, why were you following me?"

"I thought you might know." He finishes the water and looks at me with big eyes.

"Know what?" I ask.

"Where do soldiers go when the war is over?"

"They go home."

"What if you don't have a home?" he asks, shoulders hunched.

The question hits me hard. This dog was my enemy, but now I feel sorry for him.

He glances toward the Mercedes. "I envy you," he says. "You have people who care about you."

I hear a whistle and look back to find Junebug walking toward us.

"Stay in the car," I warn her.

"I was listening," Junebug says, tapping the black bud in her ear.

"That's a Maelstrom earbud," the Finisher says in amazement.

"Universal translator," Junebug says.

The Finisher stares at her, and I see recognition in his eyes. "You're General Rupani's daughter."

She nods and walks past me. She stands in front of the Finisher, unafraid despite knowing what he's capable of.

"You need a place to stay for a while, right?" she asks point-blank.

The Finisher mumbles something unintelligible.

"I know you specialize in scary whispering, but I didn't hear what you said," Junebug tells him.

"I said yes."

"My aunt's got plenty of room," Junebug says.

"Wait—" I start to say, but she holds up a hand to stop me.

"My father ran the lab that created you, Wild, and he created the Finisher, too."

She's telling the truth. We're dogs from the same home, both of us developed in the Maelstrom genetics lab.

"My family owes you one," Junebug says to the Finisher. "My father's not around to pay his debts. But I can pay them."

"You're inviting me to live with you?" he says, his voice quivering.

"Why not?" Junebug says. "It looks like you could use a good meal."

The Finisher blinks tears out of his eyes. He lopes toward her, his head rising. She gives him a good scratch between the ears.

"You could use a bath, though. No offense."

"Sorry about the smell," the Finisher says. "I've been on my own for a while."

"Do you know what you're doing?" I ask Junebug.

"I know exactly what I'm doing," she says. "I'm putting my aunt's huge place to good use." She claps her hands together and points two fingers at the Mercedes. "Let's get a move on, people. And dogs."

Before I know it, we're on our way, Junebug driving with the Finisher next to her in the front seat, and Chance and me in the back. We pull onto Olympic Boulevard, and the Finisher rolls down the window and sticks his head out, opening his mouth to the wind.

"It's been a long time since I did this!" he shouts happily.

JUNEBUG DROPS US OFF AT CHANCE'S APARTMENT COMPLEX.

We stand next to the car, staring at her through the driver's side window.

"No sentimental stuff," Junebug warns. "It's not goodbye this time. It's 'see you soon.'"

"Fine, whatever," Chance says.

"But thanks for saving my life back there, Chance. You're a good friend."

He shrugs. "You saved me a few times in the past."

"Whatever. I'm not keeping score."

"I am," Chance says. "I've saved you three times; you've saved me twice."

She laughs, and then she turns to me, her expression serious. "What happened to Dr. Pao?"

I think about the Uber driver rushing past me toward Dr. Pao. "It's a story for another time," I say.

"Promise you'll tell me everything."

"I promise," I say.

I don't want to worry Junebug right now, but the thought of Dr. Pao and the Puppio technology in CAT's hands is going to keep me up at night.

Junebug reaches a hand through the window and touches the side of my face. I give her a good lick.

"I'm really glad you're back," she says.

A final pat on my head, and then she looks over her shoulder at the Finisher. "Are you gonna keep that window down the whole drive? It's getting cold."

"Just five more minutes," he begs.

She sighs, guns the engine, and then she's gone.

I stand with Chance outside the apartment complex, shivering in the cool night air.

"How will you explain being gone to your mom?" I ask.

"I'll tell her you pushed me into a car wash, then I was held hostage against my will, then I fought my way to freedom while you took down Puppio. Or maybe I'll say I was at the school library and I lost track of time."

"Probably a better idea."

"What do you think happened to Dr. Pao?" he asks.

"Don't know exactly. She's gone for now."

"But she'll be back?"

"I'm sure of it."

I look wistfully toward the apartment, shifting from paw to paw.

I notice Chance is uncomfortable, too. He's clenching and unclenching his fists. The streetlights in the neighborhood snap on, surrounding us in a golden glow.

"What about your puppies?" Chance asks.

I wince at the painful memory.

"They're confused and they don't know who to believe. I guess they're like me when I worked for Maelstrom."

"Do you love them?"

I think about the question. Scarlett and Sebastian walking away from me, following Dr. Pao's orders, and now free in the world with the ability to control Puppio puppies. They're troubled young dogs, and they may even be dangerous.

But how do I feel about them?

"Yes. I love them," I tell Chance.

"Like I love my mom," he says. "Even though she's messed up and she does a lot of stuff that hurts."

"Like that," I say.

"Then you'll try to get them back?"

"If I can."

Chance stares up at his apartment. The lights are on, and his mother walks past the window, pacing as she talks animatedly on the phone.

"She's probably worried about you," I say.

His eyes are red and puffy, and I can see he's holding back tears.

He glances at the apartment again. "You're not coming inside with me, are you?"

I shake my head. "Puppio will be back, and they'll come after me. Besides, you have things to do. New school, new friends, and what's the name of your soccer team?"

"Santa Monica Waves."

He chews at his lower lip.

I'm memorizing every inch of him. His smell, the shaggy

hair around his eyes, the way he stands straight and holds his arms tight by his sides, making him appear older than he is.

"I guess I'd better get home," he says softly.

"Yeah."

He hesitates and taps his ear. "I'm going to keep the earbud this time," he says. "In case you ever need to talk to me."

"I never want to stop talking to you," I say.

Chance sniffles and wipes a tear from his eye. I want to run to him and bury my face in his chest to comfort him. But I stay where I am, knowing it will only make it harder to walk away.

"Okay, then," he says. "See you around, Wild."

"See you, Chance."

I start across the parking lot, willing my paws forward one step at a time.

"Wait!" Chance shouts.

I look back. Chance is bounding toward me, tears running down his cheeks.

"You can't go." He throws his arms around me, hugging me tight.

"What about the video that Puppio released? Animal Control will be searching for me."

"We'll groom you and dye your fur. People barely know what their own dogs look like, much less anyone else's."

"It will be dangerous. And Puppio's not going away anytime soon."

"I can take care of myself. I proved it, didn't I?" He looks at me expectantly.

"You did," I say with a laugh.

"Maybe we can take care of each other for a while," Chance says. "What do you say?"

"It'll be fun to dye my fur. I think I'll look better as a blond."

He smiles wide, his face bursting with joy. I leap up and lick his cheeks. He laughs as he grabs me around my midsection and pulls me close.

"I can't believe you're going to stay," he says.

"Me either." I bark with delight.

"Come on!" he says, and he runs toward the stairs, slapping his thigh to get me to keep up with him.

We rush up the stairs side by side. He stops at the top.

"One more thing," he says suddenly. "I was thinking about your kids."

"What about them?"

"If you're their mother, who's their father?"

I stop midstep. It's a question I hadn't thought about until now.

"I don't know," I say honestly.

"You should find out," he says.

"You're right. I can't believe I didn't think of that."

Sebastian and Scarlett never mentioned their father. Is it possible they don't know who he was? Or maybe they know and they kept it a secret from me. Either way, it's a mystery for me to figure out.

Later.

Right now we turn the corner to Chance's apartment. The odor of roast chicken wafts under the door and spreads down the hall.

"Do you smell that?" I ask.

"Totally. And I'm starved."

He pauses with a hand on the front door and looks down at me. "Are you ready?"

I nod.

Chance opens the door and calls into the apartment, "Mom! We're home!"

ACKNOWLEDGMENTS

Special thanks to Samantha Gentry and the team at LBYR for giving Wild a great new home. And thanks to Sarah Davies, again and always.

Doug Hill

ALLEN ZADOFF

is the author of *Wild & Chance* as well as seven books for teens and adults including the award-winning thriller series Boy Nobody/ The Unknown Assassin, which has been optioned for feature film by Overbrook Entertainment and Sony Pictures. Allen's other novels include *Food, Girls, and Other Things I Can't Have*, winner of the Sid Fleischman Humor Award from SCBWI and a YALSA Popular Paperback for Young Adults. Allen invites you to visit him at allenzadoff.com or @allenzadoff.

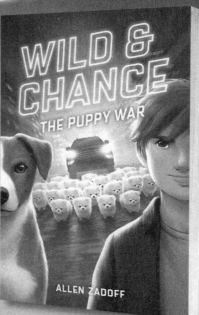